# A KISS FOR CHRISTMAS

*Holiday short stories*

## CAROLINE LINDEN

Caroline Linden

This is a work of fiction. Any references to historical events, real people, or real locales are used fictitiously. Other names, characters, places and incidents are the product of the author's imagination, and any resemblance to actual events, locales or persons, living or dead, is entirely coincidental.

# CONTENTS

# HAPPY CHRISTMAS TO ALL...

Most of these short stories were written for a yearly event at the blog Ramblings from this Chick.

Two stories (*What a Woman Needs for Christmas* and *A Scot of Her Own*) are epilogues to novels of mine, but the others are completely independent stories.

*A Kiss for Christmas* is all new for this collection, and is related to my Scandals series.

# BEL ASTRE QUE J'ADORE

*A lonely French courtesan discovers the mysterious English spy who saved her from the guillotine cares much more deeply for her than she even dreamt of…*

I t was late when the guests left, after midnight. Celeste stood on the step, waving merrily, a smile on her face, until the last gentleman had driven away in his carriage. Only then did she close the door against the light but steady fall of snow. "It is cold out," she declared, going back into the sitting room.

"Come by the fire." Rowland pulled a chair up to the fender and waited, expectant.

Still shivering, Celeste gave in and went to take the seat. "You are too good to me," she said, gratefully holding out her hands to the fire.

"You don't have to see them off from the doorway. Englishwomen wouldn't do so, not on the coldest night of the year." Rowland crossed the room to a dark corner. He had already put out most of the lamps, and now there was only the glow of the fire and the lamps on either side of the door.

It was time to go to bed, but Celeste lingered, savoring the heat on her skin. It would be almost as cold upstairs as it was outside, even though Rowland had sent the girl to light the fires upstairs. "It is my way, even if your England is too cold for it. I cannot change everything about myself."

He was quiet for a moment, then came forward. Without asking permission he draped a shawl over her shoulders—not the delicate lacy one she had worn earlier, when her parlor was full of gentlemen, but a thick, warm shawl made of wool. She made a face even as she burrowed into the comforting bulk of it. All her French notions of fashion were being abused and undermined here in the cold climate of London. Still, there was no one who could see her looking so dowdy, and she leaned back and let her eyes close.

"I haven't asked you to change anything about yourself." Rowland spoke in a low voice.

Celeste opened her eyes in surprise. He wasn't looking at

3

her, but was winding the mantel clock. He was so absorbed in everything he did, she thought; he didn't merely turn the key, he listened for the click of the mechanism. He adjusted the hands minutely. He wiped a smudge off the glass face before closing it, and then he stored the key behind the clock, where it would always be conveniently at hand. He left nothing to chance, but completed each step methodically and meticulously—not just in clock winding, but in everything.

And it had saved her life.

"You have," she replied gently to his denial. "You ask me to stay by the fire when I would stand on the step. You ask me to wear this duvet of a shawl"—she flapped one corner of it without exposing her bare shoulders to the chill of the room—"when I prefer a scrap of silk and lace. You would have me become sensible and *English*."

"I would have you live a long, healthy life." He didn't face her but continued polishing the brass fittings on the clock. The fire cast a glow upon his profile, his prominent nose, the hard line of his jaw, the surprisingly sensual shape of his mouth.

That mouth, incongruously set in such a grim and forbidding face, had been the first thing she really noticed about him, and tonight she found herself looking at his lips almost wistfully.

"Thanks to you, I shall," she murmured. "You saved me, Monsieur Rowland, from the butchers in Paris. I am forever grateful."

A muscle in his jaw flexed, and released. "It was my duty."

"To be in Paris was your duty," she agreed. He had been an army officer attached to the British Embassy, ordered to help as many Englishmen escape as possible when the republic became a charnel house. Behind fans and handkerchiefs, as France slid into hysteria, Rowland's name had been whispered as the man to look to for help.

Celeste never would have done so, even though she admired the stern, taciturn Englishman who seemed to have the trick of making himself invisible to the *sans-culottes*. She was merely a rich man's plaything, below the attentions of the English. He had spirited her neighbors—the sister of an English nobleman and her French husband—to safety, and then, unexpectedly, he had come for her. She had already begun packing for prison when he appeared at her window one night, one finger to his lips and his hand outstretched. Celeste still didn't even know why she had taken his hand and followed him into the night without a backward glance.

"To save me... Ah, that, I think, was the act of a soft heart. Or perhaps a soft head?" She tilted her head and smiled. She spoke fluent English—one of her first lovers had been an English duke, years ago—but she was still learning the English expressions. They amused her to no end.

And Rowland was so amusing to tease. As always, he frowned and gave her a severe look. "How could I leave you? They would have sent you to the guillotine."

"Perhaps."

"And would you have gone willingly if they had come for you? Would you have mounted the scaffold with a smile on your lips and a kind word for your executioner?"

"If one must die, can it not be with grace and dignity, rather than sniveling and groveling for mercy that would never come?" She gave a slight shrug, unruffled by his harsh tone. "I would not have given the crowd such a spectacle. It would hurt to smile, yes, but then the hurt would end."

His shoulders fell. "I could not have borne that," he said very quietly.

"You need not have seen it."

"I would have felt it, whether I saw it or not."

The fervor in his voice touched her. "You are so good to me, Rowland. What would I do without you?"

He shot her an odd glance. She raised an eyebrow. Rowland had been very odd this evening. He had glowered at her callers and now he was lingering longer than usual.

Celeste got to her feet. She didn't feel tired, but restless and out of sorts. Outside a carriage drove past, its wheels clacking over the cobbles. She went to the window and pulled back the drape to glance out. The clear white light of the moon sparkled on the hoarfrost that coated everything in sight. It was beautiful in its own way, she supposed, this quiet little street on the outskirts of London.

Behind her he cleared his throat. "I didn't like the company tonight."

"You never like them."

"No," he agreed bluntly. "They're all toads. You should not encourage them."

Her fingers tightened on the plush velvet of the drape. It was his, paid for by him; she knew it, though he wouldn't admit it. He had never told her who owned this house he had brought her to when she had nowhere else to go, but she was sure it was his. He moved about it with the air of a man in possession, even though he left every night. She couldn't live forever on his charity.

"It is all I know," she said softly. "I am too old to learn a trade. I am a useless ornament, nothing more." She adjusted the thick shawl more securely around her shoulders, no longer even pretending she didn't want it. She had never been this cold when she was younger. "And not even that for much longer."

"Don't say that," he said at once.

"No?" She touched the sprig of holly and ivy that deco-rated the window. He had insisted on them, for the Christmas season, and in return she had insisted on candles. She missed Christmas in Paris, even if the Paris she knew was gone. "Have I lost my bloom already?"

"Not at all."

"I will, you know," she went on. "I must make an effort to attract a new lover before I am wrinkled and stooped, for then I would be a burden on you forever."

"You are not a burden," he said quietly.

"Am I not?" She turned and swirled her hand about, like a

ballet dancer about to make her obeisance to the audience. "No one sent you to save me. I have no friends in England, no patron who will support me. I know only one way to live. All this… You pay for it, do you not?"

He said nothing.

"You brought me to London not because the English wanted it, but because you wished it." Still he made no reply. Celeste let the curtain fall and crossed the room. "You risked your life to return for me, didn't you? Why?"

Gently he reached out and took her hand. "Never say you are a useless ornament," he murmured. His fingers stroked hers. "You helped three women escape the tribunals by seducing the officer sent to arrest them and drugging his men."

"They were girls—mere children."

"One of them was rumored to be the mistress of the duc de Rochfort, with a fortune in jewels sewn in her corset."

"She earned them," said Celeste simply.

He traced the pale web of veins in her wrist with one finger. "You refused the overtures of Joseph Fouchet."

She tried to tug her hand loose. "He is a criminal."

Rowland looked up at her. She had never thought to see that look in a man's eyes when he looked at her. "He is a dangerous man. Because of him you were on the list to be arrested."

Her heart seemed to be choking her. "Was I? That must tell you what sort of man he is, if he would condemn a woman for her refusal."

"I already knew what sort of man he was." He lowered his gaze to her hand. His sensual mouth pulled taut. "I could not leave you to the likes of him."

Yes, he probably had known. Just as she knew what sort of man Rowland was. Just as she realized only now what sort of woman she might become, thanks to him.

"Monsieur Rowland." Hardly aware of what she did,

Celeste raised her free hand and touched his face, her thumb barely brushing the corner of his lips.

He inhaled like a drowning man surfacing for air. "Madame..."

"Do you not know my name? All these months you have been my constant solace and friend, and I have never heard you say it." He said nothing, but his grip on her hand tightened. "I did not like the gentlemen tonight, either," she confessed. "I have not liked one of them. I tried to tell myself it was because they are English, and very strange to me, but I fear they are simply not *you*."

His eyes were dark with tormented hope. "You owe me nothing."

She touched his mouth again. "It is not mere gratitude I feel."

"I don't want to be one of your protectors," he said. "I would rather have none of you than only part of you."

Something inside her chest quivered. "But you already have part of me."

He tensed, looking uncertain. She tried to smile, and a sprig of mistletoe caught her eye, hanging from the chandelier above their heads. She had put it up, and then spent the entire evening avoiding it—until now. "Will you give me a kiss?" she asked with forced lightness. "For Christmas?"

He glanced up, and got to his feet. He towered over her, as harsh and imposing as ever, except for the softness in his expression. "I want to marry you. Will you have me?"

"If you will kiss me," she whispered, swaying on her toes.

"Once I kiss you, I shan't stop until morning," he told her. Her lips parted. "Perhaps not even then."

"Oh, my," she breathed. The quivering inside her grew harder. "Yes."

"Yes?" He frowned, grasping her shoulders and scrutinizing her face. "Yes?"

"Yes. I am in love with you!" She smacked his chest with

her fist. "I cannot keep looking for another gentleman when all I think of is you!"

Slowly his beautiful mouth eased into a smile, and her heart gave an answering leap. "Happy Christmas, my Celeste," he murmured, and finally he kissed her.

# MY TRUE LOVE GAVE TO ME

*It's the first Christmas together for newlyweds Adam and Sarah Milbank. With a busy inn to run, they don't have much time alone with each other, until a snowstorm gives them a holiday to remember…*

Her nose was numb.

Unwilling to open her eyes, Sarah Milbank tilted her chin, thinking to tuck her nose beneath the warm blanket. Unfortunately that only alerted her to the frost on the edge of the blanket. She pried open one eye with a groan.

The old latch on the casement had slipped again, letting the window blow open. Just a bit, but enough to allow a fine silt of icy snow to blow through and settle on the bed.

"Adam," she mumbled. "The window's open."

Her husband stirred. "It's not dawn yet."

"But the window is open." She remained where she was, burrowed into the warmth of his side. Adam was a tall, strapping man, and he put off more heat than the kitchen fire.

He rolled over and threw one arm over her. "If I have to get out of bed to fix it, I'll wake up."

"I know." She sighed, trying not to think of starting the day early. "But it's snowing."

His breathing was soft and deep, and for a moment she thought he'd gone back to sleep. She was strongly tempted to do the same. "Do you think it's deep?"

She smiled, rubbing her cheek against the bare skin of his chest, where his nightshirt fell open. Her nose was not cold now. "I'd have to look out the window to guess."

"If I open my eyes and it's dark, we're staying here," he muttered. "Agreed?" His hand stroked down her back, urging her closer against him.

"Agreed." She hooked her knee over his.

There was a moment of silence. Then Adam raised his head. "Sarah, the snow is almost covering the bottom panes."

She groaned again. "Perhaps the wind blew it."

"Then there must be a fair amount of it to blow about." He

13

squeezed her hip before rolling over and sliding out of bed. "Damn, it's cold!"

She huddled under the blankets, but all the heat had gone with him. Reluctantly she opened her eyes, squinting in the dim light of early dawn. Adam walked stiff-legged around the bed, his breath hissing with every step on the frigid floorboards, and slammed the window shut, forcing the broken latch closed. "I've got to fix that," he said, for the twentieth time.

"I know." She took a deep breath and threw back the blankets. "It's freezing!"

Adam was already stepping into his trousers and rolling thick wool socks up his feet. "You can stay abed a while."

"No, I'm awake now." Teeth chattering, she snatched up a shawl and flung it around her shoulders, slipping behind the screen to wash up. There was a crust of ice over the water in the pitcher, and she was shivering by the time she had finished washing. She heard the door open as Adam left, heading out to check the livestock, no doubt. Sarah sighed, casting a bittersweet glance at the bed before rushing to put on her own warm clothes.

When she had straightened the bedroom and swept up the snow that had come through the window, she went downstairs. The Queen's Head was quiet today; no guests had stayed last night, which meant she only had to cook breakfast for herself and Adam. Even Minnie, the girl who helped in the kitchen, had gone home for Christmas. Adam had worried it was softhearted to let the girl leave a day early—what if an influx of travelers appeared unexpectedly?—but Sarah thought she could manage without her, so Minnie went.

And now, as she stirred up the fire in the big kitchen fireplace, she was glad. It had been a long time since she and Adam were alone. The Queen's Head was a small inn, but Adam hoped it would grow. Traveling coaches stopped in four times a day in good weather. They didn't get the mail coaches, which went to The Dog and Thistle a mile up the road, but they ran a cleaner establishment with better cooking, or so Adam boasted.

Sarah always blushed when he said that, but she was elated that her husband was proud of her. An innkeeper's wife's cooking could make an inn's reputation.

The kitchen warmed up quickly as she fed the fire. She filled the kettle from the hand pump Adam had installed over the summer—such a convenience, to have the pump inside the kitchen—and ground the coffe. Adam would be frozen by the time he returned from the morning chores.

She paused on that thought. It was terribly cold out, but it was also the day before Christmas. They had no guests, and judging from the depth of the unexpected snow outside the kitchen door, they weren't likely to get any. A smile curved her mouth. Yes, she would show Adam how good a cook she was today.

She flew about the kitchen gathering supplies. It was a far richer breakfast than they usually ate, but today felt deserving. She hummed a tune as she cored apples, cut slices off a leg of ham, and diced dried herbs. All was almost ready when Adam tromped through the door, shaking snow from his shoulders and boots. He handed her a basket of fresh eggs from the barn, then paused, raising his head like a hound on the scent.

"Bless my soul," he breathed, his blue eyes brightening. "Do I smell…?"

She nodded, hardly able to contain her delight. "Baked apples." She took the eggs and cracked a few into the bowl she'd prepared. "With omelette and ham."

"Breakfast for a king!" He shrugged out of his coat and hung it up, coming to the table with a look of eager anticipation on his face. "Who's arrived? Do I need to carry up luggage?"

"No." She poured the beaten eggs into the pan, sprinkled

the herbs on top, and took the coffee pot off its hook. "This is just for my husband."

"That lucky bloke!" He grinned as he straddled the bench and warmed his hands at the fire. "He'll eat me out of house and home."

She laughed. "It's our first Christmas as man and wife. I wanted it to be special."

His face softened, and he caught her around the waist as she passed with a plate of warmed ham. "I hope it is, Sarah. I know 'tis not easy being an innkeeper's wife. You were a brave soul to accept me. If we can turn a bit of profit this year, I'll hire another girl to help with the cleaning—"

She put her finger on his lips. "I'm not sorry I married you," she said softly. "Now let me serve you a Christmas breakfast befitting the keeper of the finest inn in Yorkshire."

"I intend to enjoy it more than the King himself could."

And he did. They ate ham, salty and juicy with a spoonful of saved gravy. The omelette was tender and fragrant with summer herbs from the walled garden behind the kitchen. But it was the baked apples that made Adam's eyes droop closed in happiness.

"If I hadn't already married you," he said as he polished off the last bite, "I would fall to my knees right now and beg for your hand, after such a feast."

She was ridiculously pleased. Too often they ate separately, Adam in the public room out front, seeing to guests, and she in the kitchen, a few bites at a time between tending a roast or kneading bread or baking a pie.

"The snow is fairly deep. I doubt we'll have any travelers today." He wiped one finger around the edge of his plate and licked it, a blissful expression on his face.

"No?"

He shook his head. "It's up to my knees and still drifting down. I daresay we'll be quiet for a day or more."

"Oh." She sat for a moment in growing jubilation. A day

free! They never had days free—and it was almost Christmas, too.

"I hope it clears soon." Adam went to the window and peered out. "We can't go many days without guests."

Oh yes. That tempered her delight. Adam had inherited The Queen's Head from his uncle, but he'd taken out a mortgage to make repairs and modernizations. They couldn't afford idle days.

Still, if one was forced upon them... She rose from the table. "Let's not worry about it now. I'll tidy the kitchen, you do the main room, and then we'll..." She waved one hand.

"Do what?" he prompted.

Sarah grinned. "Have a spot of fun!"

A slow smile curved his mouth. "You'll have to show me how."

So she did. Sarah rushed through the kitchen chores, then wrapped herself in her winter cloak and mittens. She went out into the kitchen yard, strangely quiet in the drifting snow, devoid of the chickens who usually strutted about. There was no rumble from the road. Everything was blanketed in white, and it seemed she and Adam must be the only people in this corner of the world.

By the time her husband came out, muffled in his own coat and hat, she was ready. As he squinted into the snow, she crouched behind the rail fence and lobbed the first snowball.

It landed on his left shoulder. He let out a startled shout.

She threw another one, trying to stifle her laughter. This one caught him on the crown of his hat as he swung around looking for her.

"An ambush!" He fell to his knees and began packing his own snowball.

"It's not a battle!" she called back, ducking behind the fence again.

"Then stand and face fire!" A snowball burst against the rail in front of her. Blindly Sarah tossed another of her own, gasping with laughter as the cold air stung her cheeks. She hadn't played like this since she was a girl, free of cares about how much beef to buy, whether they could afford a second maid to help clean, if they could make a success of The Queen's Head when it was so close to The Dog and Thistle. Snow showered down on her, and she shrieked as it slid under the collar of her cloak.

"A lady who doesn't guard her flank will be taken prisoner!" Adam leapt over the fence and snatched her into his arms as she shrieked again. "What say you now, madam?"

Sarah put one snowy mitten on his cheek. Adam was a handsome fellow, tall and broad-shouldered with fair hair and eyes of summer sky blue. She could hardly believe that he'd married her, even though he'd made no secret of the fact that her cooking skills were part of her charm. An innkeeper needed a wife who could work. She knew he held her in affection, and he treated her well, but in the six months since they'd married, she'd fallen helplessly in love with him.

"I say Happy Christmas, husband," she whispered, and then impulsively she kissed him.

It was far from their first kiss, but it might have been the first one not given in the dark privacy of their marriage bed. Even during the year of his courtship they hadn't been this silly together.

He stared at her a moment, obviously startled. Then his eyes darkened and he kissed her back, neither lightly nor quickly. Slowly her arms went around his neck as she fell into the joy of being held and kissed by the man she loved.

"Sarah," he whispered when he raised his head. "I knew it was a hard life I asked you to take on when you accepted me. But I want you to know… I'm very glad you did. You're the finest wife I could imagine, and I—"

"I love you," she blurted out, then blushed as he jerked in surprise. "I love you, Adam Milbank, and I'm glad to be your wife."

He started to grin, and then he threw back his head and

laughed. "Then this is a very happy Christmas, indeed! I'm trying to tell you I love you, too."

She gaped. "You do? Truly?"

He kissed her. "Even more than baked apples."

And then it was Sarah's turn to laugh, even though tears were stinging her eyes and snowflakes were collecting on her nose. "Then it's a good thing there's no one requesting a room today, isn't it?"

He scooped her into his arms. "Indeed it is. We ought to take advantage of it." And he carried her though the snow, into the snug little inn, and closed the door behind them.

# ADESTE FIDELES

*Marianne, Lady Fitzhugh, does not like her neighbor, retired Army officer Arthur Winston or his dog—until a chance meeting in the park on Christmas Eve, and a serenade from the smitten major.*

CHRISTMAS EVE

Marianne stopped beside the front door, tugging on her gloves. "Please look out, Farley."

Her butler paused. "Again, madam?" There was a thread of weary reluctance in his voice.

"Yes," she replied firmly. Always. Any time there was a chance *he* would be out there, terrorizing the square with his giant monster of a dog. At her feet, her own dog, sweet little Daisy, sat waiting patiently, her dark eyes trained on the door. Daisy loved walking in the square. Even though it was cold and windy out, even though it was Christmas Eve, Daisy deserved her walk.

Farley opened the door. Daisy leapt to her feet, but stayed where she was at Marianne's murmured command. Bracing himself against the wind, Farley stepped out, looking to the left. Almost immediately he stepped back across the threshold. "I see no sign of Major Winston."

Marianne sighed in relief. "Let's go, Daisy," she told her pet. The dog was already wagging her slim tail in anticipation. Marianne pulled up the fur-trimmed hood of her cloak, took firm hold of the lead, and went out into the freezing twilight. The streets were quiet, as everyone had retreated from the raw weather to the warmth of hearth and home. Ranged around St. James Square, windows glowed with light, and the faint smell of roasting meat perfumed the sharp, cold air.

Marianne led Daisy across the street and unlatched the gate enclosing the garden at the heart of the square. Today it was deserted. Marianne leaned down and unfastened the lead from Daisy's collar, and the puppy bounded away. Marianne smiled; the dog's delight was infectious. As long as she watched Daisy lope around the square, investigating every desiccated shrub with her slim, elegant nose, she could ignore the fact that her windows were mostly dark.

She had been a widow for two Christmases now.

She wasn't terribly sorry to be alone this year. Last year William's death had been too recent for her to want company. This year her sister had invited her to come to Cambridgeshire, but Marianne had demurred. It was a long, trying journey by coach. The roads were awful in winter. She had Daisy for company. Really she would enjoy a peaceful holiday at home.

Provided, of course, that her noxious neighbor Major Winston didn't ruin it.

Just thinking of him made her frown. He had taken the house two doors down from hers this summer. He was a tall, imposing figure of a man, and Mrs. McAllen, her neighbor on the other side, had told her he was something of a hero. "He captured ever so many Frenchman in the war," Mrs. McAllen had related in breathless, admiring tones. "They say he made a pretty fortune, too."

When he'd doffed his hat to her in passing one day, Marianne has even thought him rather handsome, with chiseled features and clear green eyes. For a few days she had been more than a little interested in making his acquaintance.

But then he'd brought his monstrous dog into the square. She didn't know what sort of dog it was, but he was huge.

He was covered in deep brown shaggy fur and looked as powerful as a lion, with a bark that echoed 'round the square.

The major routinely took this horrid beast with him everywhere. From her drawing room windows Marianne had watched the dog frighten teams of horses, knock over children, and splash wildly in the small fountain at the center of the square. And the major had only laughed. She could still hear his rich, deep laughter as he called the dog out of the fountain.

Worst of all, though, was that the major had allowed his dog to chase Daisy. Farley had taken Daisy out one day while Marianne had callers. A flurry of barking had sent all the ladies running to the window just in time to see the butler rush back across the street, looking quite flustered and dragging poor Daisy almost off her feet. He had burst into the house with an exclamation of ire: "Madam, Major Winston's dog is a menace!" he'd announced, thrusting the lead back into her hand. "That beast attacked us!"

Marianne's opinion of Major Winston had fallen precipitously, but she'd tried to be fair. When she encountered him on the street a day later, he strode right up to her.

"Is the little greyhound yours?" he asked very directly.

Anticipating an apology, Marianne replied, "She is."

The man's expression grew hard. "Your man tried to kick my dog when he was out with her the other day. I won't abide that."

Marianne's mouth dropped open. "Sir—"

"If you don't wish to be troubled by a dog, don't keep one," he added rudely. "They aren't ornaments."

"I never said they were!" she protested.

"Then don't treat them so cavalierly." He paused then, giving her a swift appraisal while Marianne gaped at him in stunned silence. What nerve, what arrogant presumption. What on earth did one say to that? How dare he!

And before she could think of an appropriately scathing

retort, he added, in a tone of some bemusement, "You don't look like a cruel person."

That ruined what was left of her charity with him. She'd snapped her mouth closed and stalked away, too furious to say another word. From then on she had taken great care not to cross his path, even if it meant delaying her departure or taking a different route away from home. For the last month, she'd hardly left her house without making Farley check first that the major was nowhere to be seen.

Without meaning to, she glanced toward his house as she strolled the gravel path that circled the garden. A few windows were lit, but nothing to indicate a festive gathering. Of course there wouldn't be, she told herself, huddling into her cloak as the wind picked up. A bachelor would likely be with family, instead of the other way around. She hadn't seen him for a few days; perhaps he'd left London and would be away for some time. The thought of being able to come and go at will made her shoulders ease. It would quite make up for spending the Christmas season at home alone.

## ❧ 2 ❧

Arthur Winston spent several minutes debating whether or not he could just let Pilot out alone.

Arguing for it was the freezing temperature outside, with a wind that made the windows in the front parlor rattle. Arthur had spent too many nights in miserable army camps to want another minute in the winter chill, even a short walk to the garden across the street. He had a blazing fire in his hearth and a glass of brandy to enjoy, as well as a good book.

What's more, the weather wouldn't bother Pilot at all. The big dog had been bred by fisherman, and Arthur had seen his breed plunge into icy waters to save those washed overboard. There was little traffic on the streets, for most people were buttoned up at home for Christmas Eve. All in all, it was probably entirely safe to open the door and let the dog out to relieve himself.

Pilot was pacing the front hall, the telling sign that he really needed to go out. Arthur stepped to the window overlooking the square and opened the shutter. If there were no carriages anywhere in sight, he told himself, he'd do it.

No clatter of wheels, not even a passing hackney. He

sighed in relief, just as his gaze snagged on a lone figure strolling the garden.

He leaned closer to the glass, squinting. It was a woman, in a bright red cloak with her hands in a muff. *A bit mad*, he thought, reaching for the shutter. But then a small pale gray dog dashed through the shrubbery and began leaping around her, and his hand paused.

The woman stopped and bent down to pet the dog, her head tilting to one side. The wind lashed at her cloak, and a long dark curl blew free before she tucked it back into the confines of the hood.

Arthur banged the shutter shut and strode into the hall. "I know, I know," he told his restless dog as he jammed his arms into his greatcoat. He cursed under his breath as he searched for his gloves, finally locating them beneath his hat. With only one glove on and his hat in hand, he threw open the door, barely feeling the cold as Pilot rushed out only slightly faster than he did.

He meant to apologize, he told himself as he crossed the street. Lady Fitzhugh had moved out of sight by the time he pushed open the gate to the garden. Arthur buttoned his coat, regretting his forgotten scarf as the wind howled, and scanned the garden for his elusive but lovely neighbor. He had a feeling he'd offended her.

Well, he knew he had—not intentionally, but her manservant had cursed and kicked at Pilot, then dragged the poor little greyhound away by the neck. Arthur could tell when a man had no feeling for animals, and he'd let his temper get away from him when he confronted the lady about her servant's treatment of both dogs.

Shoulders hunched, he paced the path. She couldn't have left the garden; he had a perfect view of the gate opposite her door. After their disastrous conversation, which ended with her gazing at him in shocked affront, he'd learned a little more about her. A widow whose husband had died two years ago. She still lived quietly, not reclusively, but every day she walked her dog, whom she loved dearly.

He'd hoped to run into her again, after his temper had cooled and he'd decided she probably had no idea her man was too rough with her pet, but in the month since that unfortunate meeting, he'd only seen her through the window or from afar.

And that, he realized, was not enough. Lady Fitzhugh was very attractive. She was petite but curvy, with a sweetly shaped figure he admired far too much. She had big brown eyes and a luscious pink mouth, which had sparked several indecent ideas in his mind. Not for the first time he wished he'd been born with a more diplomatic temperament. Perhaps if he'd called on her, with some flowers or something, they would be friendly neighbors. Perhaps she would smile when they met, or at least not dodge meeting him. Perhaps—

Pilot gave a playful bark somewhere to his left, just as a woman's alarmed cry reached his ears. Arthur took off at a run, hoping Pilot hadn't knocked her over. The dog weighed nearly ten stone but still behaved like a puppy. He sprinted around a pair of plane trees and saw the trouble.

"Pilot!" His dog stopped chasing the little greyhound around Lady Fitzhugh's skirts, although his tail continued to wag.

Lady Fitzhugh whipped around to glare at him, her cheeks cherry red. "Call him off!" she cried.

Arthur whistled. Pilot gave the smaller dog a last wistful glance, then trotted obediently to his side. "Are you hurt?"

"I—No, I am not hurt!" She was angry, though. "He was frightening Daisy!"

"I apologize. He's still a young dog and only wants to play. She was never in any danger."

She gave him a fulminating glance. "Appearances were very much to the contrary!" Without waiting for a reply she bent down, apparently trying to attach a lead to her dog. The greyhound seemed to have recovered from any fright Pilot had put into her. She danced around her mistress's skirts, peering at him first from one side, then the other. At Arthur's side, Pilot gave a low whimper of longing.

"Will you take that dog away?" demanded Lady Fitzhugh. She straightened and glared at him in exasperation. Her efforts had loosened more curls, and the wind tossed them around her face.

Arthur blinked out of his daze. She was beautiful—and very annoyed at him. He muttered a command and Pilot reluctantly lay down, though his eyes never left the greyhound. "He's well trained," Arthur said.

She sniffed. "Hardly! I see him all the time, romping about the square, chasing children and scaring horses."

"That's not true," he countered. "Pilot never chases children. He might have tumbled one or two to the ground, but only out of an excess of affection. He's very friendly."

Lady Fitzhugh merely frowned. Heaven help him, even that expression was appealing; it pushed her mouth into a perfect *kiss me* pout.

"I'm glad to see you walking Daisy yourself this evening," he said hastily, trying not to dwell on the fact that the two of them were the only souls in sight, alone in this sheltered corner of the garden. "You shouldn't send her out with the tall gray-haired fellow."

Her eyes flashed. "Why not?"

"He doesn't like dogs."

"Nonsense," she declared. "He's very fond of Daisy."

Arthur shrugged. "Then he's not fond of walking her. And I don't think she enjoys his care much, either."

She looked astonished, then she turned her back to him and made another effort to grab her dog. The greyhound didn't want to be caught, though; she leapt away and wagged her tail. Arthur suspected she was taunting Pilot, who still remained in place but with his attention fixed on her.

"If I give my word to call Pilot back at a moment's notice, will you let them run?" he asked cautiously. "She's far faster than Pilot, he'll never catch her if she doesn't want to be caught."

Lady Fitzhugh gave him a fulminating look. Daisy was watching Pilot, her sleek head cocked playfully, and Lady Fitzhugh took the opportunity to lunge at her.

But, as Arthur had said, the greyhound was fast. She shot away from her mistress's sudden movement and flew across the frozen grass. Unable to resist any longer, Pilot took off after her with a joyful bark.

And Arthur ran two steps forward to catch Lady Fitzhugh as she staggered and slipped. "Careful," he murmured against her dark hair. The wind had blown her hood back, and her curls smelled like cinnamon.

"Major!" Pink-cheeked, she struggled against his grip.

"You're standing on ice," he said, nodding his head toward the ground. It was true; water from the fountain had blown over the walk and formed a hard slick coating. Her wide dark eyes followed his, and she went still. "Let me just..." God, she felt lovely in his arms. More a man of action than words, he gently lifted her against him and set her feet on the grass. Reluctantly he let her go.

"Thank you." She backed up a step, looking troubled. "What did you mean earlier? About Daisy not enjoying Farley's care."

"Farley is the gray-haired fellow?"

"My butler," she replied, lifting her chin.

"I saw him yanking her about until I thought her neck would snap. He dragged her around a few bushes and then headed straight back to the house, resisting all her efforts to stop. Dogs are animals and need to be outside. Your butler clearly wanted to be inside."

"He must have been in a hurry that once," she said slowly. "He has other duties, after all..."

"I've seen him walk her a dozen times and it's always the same." Arthur hesitated. He could still feel the shape of her body against his. "Why don't you walk her yourself?"

For a split second she stared at him with... guilt. "I do," she murmured, turning away. "And I should take her in now. Daisy!"

"Have you been avoiding the square because of me?" Arthur exclaimed in astonishment, suddenly realizing why he never managed to cross paths with her.

"Of course not. Daisy!" she cried desperately. She picked up her skirts and hurried off. "Daisy!"

Arthur kept stride beside her. "Why?"

"Of course not," she protested. "But—but if you must know, it's your dog!" Pilot and Daisy were nowhere in sight. Lady Fitzhugh stopped, her breath curling in plumes around her head. "He frightens everyone, Major."

On impulse he seized her hand. "I apologize for that. I don't want you to be frightened of him... or of me."

Her eyes rounded and her lips parted. Arthur tamped down a renewed surge of appreciation. He tucked her hand around his arm. "Let me show you."

He gave a sharp whistle, and a moment later heard the thud of Pilot's paws. Flying ahead of him came Daisy, her ears back and her eyes bright.

"Daisy isn't frightened," Arthur said to the woman beside him. "Nor would Pilot hurt her. He's more inclined to rescue people—and animals—than hurt them."

The big dog plowed to a stop before them, sitting at Arthur's command. But Daisy leapt all about him, nipping at his ears and sprinting away before darting back. Her tail was wagging, and when Pilot rolled onto his back and put up his enormous paws, Daisy sprang right on top of him.

"She's playing," said Marianne numbly. She'd never seen her pet so active and obviously happy.

Major Winston nodded. "It's just as good for dogs as it is for children. She's an active little creature, I'll wager."

"Very." She couldn't say more. The dogs were playing—

and Daisy looked delighted. In spite of herself, a little laugh escaped her.

The major cleared his throat. "Are you still frightened?"

Now she felt like a fool. "No," she said softly. As if he heard her, Pilot folded his front legs around her little dog and began licking her enthusiastically on the head. And Daisy settled down as if she enjoyed it.

Major Winston shifted his weight. Marianne realized he was blocking the wind. He was a big fellow, and so warm. She had unconsciously moved closer to him as they watched the animals. "I'm unspeakably relieved, Lady Fitzhugh. I never thought that would be the reason you were avoiding me."

Her face burned. He had noticed. "I don't know what you mean, sir."

The major looked abashed. "Er. We've been neighbors for several months now but hardly meet. I wondered why."

And for the first time Marianne became exquisitely aware that they had been standing very near each other for some time now, utterly alone except for the two dogs. Up close the major was even handsomer than from a distance, and she was taken off guard by how lovely it felt to have a man's arm around her, and how masculine a man could smell. She hadn't realized how his deep voice would spark a faint buzz across her skin that could only be called attraction.

Rattled, she released his arm and stepped away. "Coincidence," she managed to say. "I should return. Daisy, come." This time her dog listened, and allowed Marianne to re-attach her lead. Feeling in control of herself again, she rose and faced the major. "Good evening, sir."

His smile was a little crooked. "Happy Christmas, Lady Fitzhugh."

"Oh—yes, Happy Christmas to you," she replied, flustered. His house lay directly behind him. The windows were as dark as the windows of her own house, only a few windows illuminated. "Are you not visiting family?" she blurted out.

"No," he said. "They are too far."

She nodded. "Of course. Mine is as well."

His hesitated, his dark eyes intent on her, and then seemed to reach a decision. "How unfortunate. 'Tis a day for family and friends."

Uncomfortably she nodded. Together they walked across the frozen garden in silence, Pilot trotting behind. Marianne's thoughts were in torment. Should she invite him to share her Christmas dinner? It did seem very lonely now to spend the whole day alone, and it would serve as apology for avoiding him. Did Farley really drag Daisy by the neck? How could she have missed that? If she had seen him doing it, she would have been just as outraged as the major had been when he spoke sharply to her.

"Well, good night," he said, snapping her out of her thoughts. They had reached her step.

Marianne blushed. "Good night, sir." On impulse, she added, "Thank you. I will speak to Farley."

Major Winston's mouth curved in a rueful smile. With his hair ruffled by the wind, he looked roguishly attractive. "Walk the dog yourself. Pilot will want to see her again."

Marianne nodded and went inside, into her parlor. Tomorrow she would speak to Farley, but tonight she couldn't stop thinking about Major Winston. He was also alone for Christmas. Her cook had a whole goose to roast for dinner tomorrow. Would it be neighborly? Would it be forward? She ran her hand over the desk near the window, and couldn't decide.

Arthur paced his parlor, unable to decide. Pilot settled in for a nap near the hearth, looking as contented as a dog could look. And no wonder—he had finally got a chance to romp with the object of his affection, Arthur thought sourly, while his master was still held at arm's length.

Perhaps that would begin to change now that he'd allayed her fears about the dog. Arthur thought she must have seen Pilot out with the Beech children, when his friend John Beech brought his family to visit. Since John's eldest boy was prone to trying to ride Pilot like a horse, no wonder the dog had knocked him down. Arthur knew for a certainty the boy wasn't hurt, and Pilot was never allowed to run wild and knock down other children.

He knew he should sit down in the chair by the fire and return to his book and brandy. But he also knew Lady Fitzhugh was alone, perhaps a little lonely as well, and he'd always been a man of action. He could still feel her in his arms, when he'd caught her on the ice. He wanted to make her laugh again, and smile, and not at the damned dogs.

On impulse, he snatched up his coat again, this time remembering his scarf. In the army they'd used to sing on

Christmas Eve, when there were few other comforts of the season to be had. People had told him he had a good voice. Pilot lifted his head as he opened the parlor door.

"Wish me luck," he told the dog, and Pilot answered with a firm *woof.*

He stopped right outside her windows. They glowed with light, and as he watched, the lady herself walked past. Her head was down and she seemed to be deep in thought. Encouraged, elated again by the sight of her, Arthur cleared his throat and began to sing.

"Adeste fideles læti triumphantes…"

By the end of the first verse, she was standing still in the middle of the room. He could just spy the top of her head, from his position on the pavement.

"Deum de Deo, lumen de lumine…"

By the end of the second verse, she had take a seat close to the window. Now he could see the lamplight gleaming on her dark curls.

"Cantet nunc io, chorus angelorum…"

He knew four verses by heart. There were more, but his memory was unreliable. At the end of the next verse, he would have to go home and wait for another opportunity. Lady Fitzhugh still sat by the window, her back to him. Was she pleased? Flattered? Appalled? Cringing at his voice? Contemplating sending her butler out to chase him away?

*A faint heart never won a lady*, he reminded himself, and plunged into the fourth and final verse.

"Ergo qui natus die hodierna.

Jesu, tibi sit gloria,

Patris æterni Verbum caro factum.

Venite adoremus

Venite adoremus

Venite adoremus

Dominum."

He had barely finished the final note when her door opened. Lady Fitzhugh herself stood in the rectangle of light, as beautiful as an angel to Arthur's eyes. He closed his mouth and bowed.

"That was lovely," she said.

He grinned. "Thank you. We used to sing in camp, during my army years, when there were no friends and family to share the season with."

"We used to sing at home." She hesitated. "Would you like to come in and sing some more? I can play the pianoforte."

And Arthur thought he heard the heavenly chorus for just a moment. "I would be delighted, Lady Fitzhugh."

# WHAT A WOMAN NEEDS
# FOR CHRISTMAS

*A surprise arrival on Christmas Eve brightens the holiday for a new*
*wife.*
*A holiday epilogue to*
What a Woman Needs

CHRISTMAS EVE

The fire had already been banked for the night and the maid had pulled the drapes closed. The old house was drafty and grew terribly cold on winter nights, especially bitter ones like tonight. A raw wind had whipped the countryside for days now, but tonight it brought freezing rain as well, needles of ice that tinkled against the window panes and hissed in the fireplace.

The lady of the house surveyed her quiet domain. She had sent the servants, all three of them, to bed early, and her niece had gone upstairs a short while ago, too. There was no point burning through a week's worth of fuel trying to keep the house warm tonight. She pulled her shawl around her shoulders and put out all but a single lamp, then took up that one to light her way to bed.

In the doorway she paused, looking back at the small sitting room. It was by far the nicest room in the house now. The windows were secure behind thick drapes, the fresh paint brightened the room considerably, and the floor had been waxed to a shine. Her niece Susan had decorated with sprigs of greenery as well, bringing in the fresh scent of the forest along with a dash of color. It would be a pleasant Christmas, even with the general shabbiness of the rest of the house.

She sighed and turned away, bracing herself for the walk upstairs. The maid had prepared her room, but it would still be cold and lonely, and there was nothing anyone could do about that.

As she reached the foot of the stairs, a sound caught her attention. She paused, frowning. It sounded like steps outside the wide front door, but who could be out on a night like this? No one, of course. It must be the storm.

But the knock that came next, a pair of short muffled thumps, was not the storm. Most likely not, at any rate. Still frowning, she set down the lamp and hurried to the door.

41

"Who is there?" she called, resting her palms on the scarred wood and listening.

For answer, there was silence. She closed her eyes and rested her forehead against the wood. It was no one, of course. The wind must have blown something against the house.

Three more knocks, solid thumps this time, made the wood beneath her forehead vibrate. A voice called out—or was it the wind?—and she hesitated, then undid the bolt and opened the door a few inches to peer out.

She barely glimpsed a man's figure before he pushed past her into the hall. His every step squelched loudly, and a steady patter of raindrops fell around him from his soaked greatcoat. Slowly, jerkily, he unwound the long, frost-covered muffler from his neck and dropped it to the floor.

Her mouth fell open as she saw his face. "What are *you* doing here?"

He grinned. A few days' growth on his jaw gave him a wild, dangerous look as he tossed aside his hat and shook his head like a dog, water and ice flying from his dark hair. "You don't sound pleased to see me."

She raised her chin. "And why should I be?"

This time he laughed. He peeled off his sodden gloves, one finger at a time, before flicking them aside with the muffler. "What a fine welcome. How can you deny a man the warmth of your hospitality on a night such as this?"

"Any man who ventures out on a night such as this is a fool," she retorted. "What do you want?"

"Oh, I'm a fool," he said comfortably. "But where is your comfort and cheer, madam? It is the Christmas season."

"I expect it's all gone out the leaking roof and the smoky chimney in the dining room."

He casted a glance into the sitting room, where the coals still glowed faintly in the grate. "But it was here. I smell evergreen. Dare I hope to find a bit of mistletoe as well?"

"You may hope all you like," she replied, "and much good might it do you."

"Ah, I see." He gave her a glance glittering with amusement. "I understand. A leaky roof, a smokey chimney ... What sort of man would leave a woman in such a hovel in winter? Your husband ought to be whipped."

She twisted her lips into a sardonic smile. "Perhaps."

His greatcoat hit the floor with a wet slap, revealing how little it had protected him from the weather. He rolled his shoulders with a grimace, then peeled off his jacket as well, tossing it onto the growing pile of his discarded clothing. His white shirt clung to powerful arms, and her eyes drifted down the broad planes of his chest before she jerked them back to his face—which wore a knowing smirk.

She turned her back on him and started for the stairs, turning her head to speak over her shoulder. "My husband is expected in a week's time. I'm sure you'll be welcome then."

He followed her. "Lucky fellow, to come home to such a beauty."

She sniffed. "Flattery will not serve you, sir."

"No?" He laughed softly, prowling ever closer to her. She quickened her step, keeping the distance between them, until he outmaneuvered her and strode around, barring her path to the stairs. "Perhaps your husband isn't lucky, then. Perhaps he's a bloody idiot for leaving you here alone in the country." She just shrugged, and his easy laugh rang out again, more confidently this time as he came toward her. "So, he *is* an idiot. Well, perhaps I can warm your heart in preparation for his return. It seems the most I can do, since I plan to take full advantage of his hearth and table tonight."

"My husband—" she said sharply. She had backed into the wall against his approach, and now made to move to the side, around him.

"You husband," he echoed, placing one hand on the wall where she would have gone, then the other hand on the other side to trap her in place.

"Yes, my husband," she snapped. "He will not like it that you're taking advantage of me this way!"

"On the contrary, my dear," he whispered, lowering his face to hers. "I think he'd approve very much." And he kissed her.

She tried to turn her face away. She grabbed at his wet shirt and tried to push him away. But slowly, inexorably, he gathered her into his arms, kissing her until her hands clutched instead of shoved, and her arms went around his neck with a soft moan of surrender.

"There," he said softly, his breath gone as ragged as hers. "I think your husband would expect me to finish that properly. Come upstairs with me."

She let her head fall back so he could kiss the length of her neck. "You wicked man, to show up like this and expect me to fall into your arms …"

"By God, yes. I'm counting on it," he murmured, sliding his hand up to cover her breast. "I'll take you straight to bed and keep you warm all night."

She shivered, both from the prospect of having him in her bed and from the touch of his hand on her flesh. Even when she wanted to refuse him, he made it impossible. It frightened her sometimes, how potent her desire for him was.

"Say yes, darling." He kissed her again, deeply. "Take pity on a poor man nearly drowned, half frozen, willing to risk his life for a night in your arms."

"You know I would say yes," she breathed as his fingertips teased her skin until she arched her back, pressing into him. "Oh, Stuart, you've been away too long …"

"Do you think I don't know that?" He cupped her cheek and gazed into her dark eyes with rueful blue ones. "Why do you think I rode through the storm tonight?"

"Because you're mad," she said with a muted laugh. "It's positively dreadful out."

He grinned. "I'm only mad for you, darling."

"But you're home early," Charlotte said. "I didn't expect you for another week. Did something happen—?"

"No, everything went well." He'd left five weeks ago to visit his grandfather, Viscount Belmaine, and try to restore some familial connection. Only this summer Stuart had learned that his supposed father was really his uncle, his presumed mother was only his adoptive mother, and that his grandfather had helped conceal the truth for decades.

Charlotte had been unsure when he declared he needed to visit Lord Belmaine, but Stuart assured her it would be fine. As his visit had lengthened, Charlotte prayed it was for good reasons and not for bad ones. She herself wouldn't have forgive such deception so easily. But Belmaine controlled the family fortune, and there was no doubt that they could use some funds.

"Not only did I persuade Grandfather to part with some of his best sheep in the spring, I ordered supplies for the new roof. He's of a mind to come and see you for himself this spring, you know. The old bounder still likes a pretty woman, and I daresay he's curious to see who could possibly have won my faithless heart. But we'll have a good flock come spring, a new roof, and perhaps—just perhaps—the dining room chimney rebuilt. All in all, a trip well worth the inconvenience." He paused and his gaze heated. "But then I thought of my beautiful wife, all alone in the wilds of Somerset—"

She scoffed. "Susan has been with me," she said, naming her niece. "I've hardly been alone."

"Alone—*desperately* lonely— in the wilds of Somerset," he repeated willfully. "Pining for my presence. No doubt crying herself to sleep every night." Charlotte laughed. "And it is our first Christmas, and I've not given you a gift."

"I don't need a gift now that you're home." Despite his wet clothing, she rested her cheek against him. "I missed you."

"And I you." His fingers brushed her cheek. "Happy Christmas, darling Charlotte."

"Happy Christmas, Stuart." She stepped back and surveyed him from head to toe. "Take off your clothes."

"Here?" His wolfish grin flashed at her as she reached for the lamp.

She smiled coyly and backed toward the stairs. "You're soaking wet. We should get you before a hot fire ... or into bed ..."

"Lord, yes." He yanked at his cravat.

Charlotte ignored the pile of wet clothing on the floor; there would be time enough to deal with that tomorrow. He'd been gone over a month, five very long and lonely weeks. Christmas had come a few hours early for her. "I shall do my best to warm you."

Her husband caught her on the stairs. "You always do, my love," he whispered against her mouth. "And always will."

———

R ead Stuart's and Charlotte's story in **What a Woman Needs.**

# A SCOT OF HER OWN

*Rosalind, Dowager Duchess of Exeter, has given up on finding romance with Lord Warfield, but he has not—even if means he must race back to London from Scotland in time for Christmas.*
*A holiday epilogue to*
A Rake's Guide to Seduction

CHRISTMAS EVE 1824

"I don't know why you invited him." Rosalind, Dowager Duchess of Exeter, stood staring out the window at the snow flurrying outside.

"He's Anthony's uncle, Mama," said her daughter. "And he would be alone in Scotland otherwise. Surely you don't wish that upon him."

Rosalind pressed her lips together, feeling churlish and anxious, which in turn made her feel guilty. It was Christmas Eve, a day for joy. "Of course not. But it is a very long journey, dear, and a man of his age—"

Celia's peal of laughter cut her off. "His age! Mama, he's barely fifty, and the heartiest gentleman I know. Do you know..." Her voice dropped although the admiring tone lingered. "Anthony says he swims every day in the River Anan. Can you imagine? I never would have put one toe into the lake in Cumberland, not even on the most sweltering day of summer, and Anandale is even further north."

Before she could stop herself, Rosalind pictured the man in question dropping his kilt and plunging into the water. "He's not long for this life, then," she said to banish the

49

image. "Encouraging him to travel in this weather may finish him off."

"I'm sure he would have written to say he could not come, if he were unwell, but he assured Anthony he would be here by Christmas."

"He may not have wanted to disappoint you." Rosalind turned and couldn't help smiling at the scene. Celia, her only daughter, was on the floor with her son, Rosalind's first grandchild. Far from keeping the baby off in the nursery, Celia seemed to have recovered some of her own carefree youth and could regularly be found playing on the floor with her baby.

Rosalind remembered her own mother counseling her to remember her station and dignity at all times, but the sight of her daughter's luminous smile crushed any impulse she might have ever had to say anything like that. Celia had endured a disastrous first marriage, ending in her widowhood at the age of twenty-two, and she'd returned home so silent and somber Rosalind had feared for her health and even her sanity.

But now... now she was married again, blissfully happily this time, with a child of her own and a husband who adored her. It was enough to make any mother smile.

If only her son-in-law hadn't had a vexingly attractive uncle, who was invited to spend Christmas with them.

The baby, Louis, had just started to sit up by himself, and now he was surrounded by a mountain of cushions, blue eyes fixed on the silver rattle his mother held. He reached for it and slowly toppled forward until he caught himself on his little hands.

Celia glanced up, her face still bright with adoration. "He's going to crawl, Mama. Look at him!" The baby rocked back and forth, still focused on the rattle Celia waved. He lifted one hand to reach for it and managed to grab it before tumbling onto his side and then his back, the rattle in his mouth.

Rosalind smiled. "You might put the rattle farther from him, in that case. He's devoted to it."

"He likes to make noise." Beaming, Celia tickled her baby's feet, and he responded with a gurgle and a kick.

The door opened and Celia's husband Anthony came in. "Warfield's arrived," he said, before catching sight of his son on the floor. "There's my fine boy!" He went down on one knee and put his arm around Celia's shoulders. "Crawling by the New Year, don't you think?"

"No, I think by Christmas," Celia replied.

"Did you say Warfield has arrived?" Rosalind interrupted, her pulse still racing.

"Yes, he rode his horse straight to the mews and needed a moment to dry off from his ride," said Anthony, not even looking up from his child. "Do you really think as soon as tomorrow, darling?"

"I do. And how wonderful that Lord Warfield will be here to see it," said Celia. "Show your papa how you shake the rattle, Louis," she cooed.

"Wonderful," murmured Rosalind. Of course she had expected him to come, but knowing he was under the same roof at this moment sent her nerves skittering wildly. "If you'll excuse me, I think I'll fetch a warmer shawl."

"Of course, Mama." Celia barely managed to look up. "Anthony, ring for someone to build up the fire. I'm sure Lord Warfield will be chilled as well."

Rosalind let herself out of the room, leaving the young family alone. Celia's new happiness brought unspeakable joy to her own heart, it truly did. But as delighted as she'd been by the birth of young Louis, his arrival had marked a distinct turning point in Rosalind's relationship with her own daughter. Rosalind had never wanted to be the sort of mother who lived only for her children, but now that her daughter, as well as her two step-sons, were married and had children of their own, she felt a bit... useless.

She started up the stairs, trying not to feel old. She ought to find a cause to patronize or a society to sponsor. That's what most women did at her stage of life: neither feeble nor infirm, but widowed and no longer responsible for children. A single dowager in possession of a good fortune must be in want of a charitable cause. She had admired those women from afar but somehow never quite thought she would be one of them before she was fifty.

Of course, the arrival of the Earl of Warfield had nothing to do with her feeling of growing old. A year ago, he had paid her some significant attention. The day Celia married Anthony, Lord Warfield had pulled her into his arms, kissed her, and asked if he could call on her. Over the next several months, he had come to call several times. They had discussed, and argued over, philosophy and politics, art and literature. They'd taken drives in the park, walks in the garden, visited the museum and attended the opera together.

For a while, Rosalind had felt like a young woman again, worrying about her hair and her wardrobe, with a suitor sending her flowers. And when Warfield told her he had to return to his property in Scotland, but would call on her when he returned and hoped to discuss something very important with her, she had even begun to imagine that his attention was serious; that he meant to propose marriage; that she would have to decide what answer to give him.

Rosalind had been gripped by a wholly inappropriate flutter of nervous excitement, awaiting his return. She had even begun to believe she would say *yes* if he came back to London and went down on bended knee and asked her to marry him. The man was vexing and opinionated but he was also good-humored and terrible attractive and he made her laugh and lie awake at nights thinking of him.

But he didn't—come back to London, that is. Throughout the summer, she'd understood; letters arrived from Scotland every fortnight assuring her he hoped to return by the end of summer, lamenting that he was still detained. By the fall, the stream of letters had trailed into a trickle; only one letter arrived. And as of this day, Rosalind hadn't heard from the earl in almost two months.

There was only one conclusions, really. He had changed his mind. Whatever interest he'd had in her had waned. Rosalind had had plenty of time to be perplexed, then annoyed, then sad, before finally accepting, and carrying on with her life.

She was a duchess, after all. She was not pining for that vexing man. She had assured Celia that they did not suit, and that her heart was unaffected. And she'd meant it.

But she did *not* look forward to seeing him at Christmas.

She hurried up the stairs, telling herself she was not trying to avoid him. She would be poised and reserved, as if he had never called on her and made her think he meant anything by it.

At the top of the stairs she turned toward the gracious suite of rooms Celia had assigned her. Perhaps she would linger there with a book… ring for a cup of tea… write some letters by the fire. There was no earthly reason for her to rush back to the drawing room; in fact, she should probably remain in her room until dinner. Let Anthony have the chance to welcome his uncle in privacy, she told herself.

And no sooner had she assured herself this was the genteel thing to do, the Earl of Warfield stepped out of the door across from hers and squarely into her path.

## 2

Patrick Murray, Earl of Warfield, had been rushing for the better part of two months, so after he'd hastily changed his coat and scrubbed his face, he charged into the corridor without looking, and nearly ran down the woman he'd been racing to see.

"Goodness!" she gasped, one hand flying to her throat.

Patrick winced. The one thing he hadn't worked out yet was exactly how to explain and apologize to her. He had told himself the words would come when he saw her, and now he realized that was a lie. "Your Grace. I beg your pardon."

Her chin came up. Rosalind, Dowager Duchess of Exeter, was possibly the finest looking woman he'd ever set eyes on. Not too tall, not too slim, he admired her from the top of her silver-blond curls to the tips of her dainty silk-shod toes, and every inch in between. He'd met her at a house party the previous year, where he took one look and felt Cupid's arrow strike him in the heart.

Even now, when he knew he probably ought to fall to his knees, just the sight of her face made him feel warm inside. She had spirit and wit and the sweetest smile when he kissed her—

"Lord Warfield." Her cool, polite tone threw ice water on

his increasingly heated thoughts. She tilted her head in the merest suggestion of a curtsy. "I trust you had a pleasant journey."

It had been terrible, riding through icy rain down rutted roads. The carriage had got stuck so many times he'd taken to the saddle in desperation, leaving his valet and baggage to muddle along behind him. Any sensible person would have stayed in Dumfriesshire until spring.

"I hardly felt a moment's discomfort," he told her, "anticipating the holiday here."

She smiled, but not that soft, tempting smile. That was the duchess's frosty curve of the lips. "Mr. and Mrs. Hamilton are expecting you in the drawing room. I shan't keep you."

No, no, no. He wanted her to keep him, very much. "Won't you walk down with me?"

"I was on my way to my rooms."

"May I escort you there?" he countered.

"That is unnecessary, sir."

"It would be my pleasure." He extended his arm hopefully.

Something flitted over her face, half annoyed, half awkward. "My room is there," she said with a delicate motion at the door across the corridor. "I believe I can manage the distance unaided."

Oh Lord. Her door was opposite his own. Patrick wasn't sure if he ought to thank or curse his host for that bit of temptation. How the devil was he supposed to sleep now, knowing she was only a few feet away?

"Well, I never thought you'd *need* my arm, even if the room lay on the other side of Mayfair," he said, abandoning all subtlety. "I was hoping you might want it. I would be very glad for a stroll with you."

Her brow went up. "It has been raining all day."

He grinned. "Has it, now? 'Tis very mild out, to a Scot."

"I am not a Scot."

"I didn't mean to walk in the garden. Just…" He looked

around. His nephew's house was spacious, for London, but that didn't mean much. "Here," he finished lamely.

"Up and down the corridor?" she asked archly.

"And the stairs, maybe." Ah, good; now she was laughing at him. He could see the smile fighting its way to her lips. Gads, she was beautiful when she smiled. "A promenade about the dining table, if the mood takes us."

"Lord Warfield," she began, her lips trembling.

"Ah, lass, don't call me that," he begged. "Call me Patrick, as you once did. Patrick You Bloody Idiot would also serve, or Patrick, Damned Fool—"

"Stop it." She took a deep breath, obviously to restore her composure. "That was a long time ago," she said evenly. "Best forgotten. You must pardon me—"

"I don't want to!"

Her brows shot up. "How rude."

"More like desperate. I know I owe you an explanation—"

"Of course you do not," she said coolly. "You owe me nothing. Anthony and Celia will be wondering what's keeping you. Go down and see them, and young Louis. They're taking sides on how soon he crawls. I have some letters to write. Until dinner, sir." With a graceful dip of her head, she moved past him and disappeared into her room.

And Patrick said a curse under his breath before going downstairs to find his nephew.


He did not see her again until dinner. That was good, he told himself. It gave him time to observe the formalities of greeting and conversing with Anthony and his wife. He didn't want to make it obvious that he'd come mainly because Anthony's invitation had mentioned that Rosalind would also be with them for Christmas.

Patrick loved his nephew and had done his best to provide familial support after his sister died, but the lad was well situated now, with a beautiful wife and a son of his own.

Anthony didn't require an uncle's company any longer. And London was far from Anandale, a trying journey in the best of weather, let alone in December.

But he'd made a monumental mistake regarding Rosalind, and Patrick thought he'd ride through a hurricane on a sheep for a chance to fix it.

There was no chance at dinner; it was only the four of them, and Patrick didn't want to explain everything in front of Anthony and Celia. But Celia excused herself from the drawing room, saying she was going to check on her son and would be back soon. Anthony gave him a quick glance before leaping out of his seat and declaring that he also wished to look in on the baby, and he whisked his wife out of the room before Rosalind could speak. Her lips, in fact, were still parted in amazement when he caught her eye.

"The baby must be fast asleep by now," she protested.

He shrugged. "They're new to this. Did you never want to look on your sleeping babe?"

"Of course, Lord Warfield. I also did not wish to *wake* the sleeping babe."

"Oh," he said. "I never thought of that. I've no children of my own, of course."

She smiled very briefly.

Patrick hesitated, then moved to sit opposite her. "May I help?" She was sorting little balls of thread.

"If you like. The greens, please."

He nodded and began picking out the coils of green. "I'm glad of a chance to talk to you alone."

"Oh?" She didn't look at him, and her tone was utterly disinterested.

"Aye. It's about Ned."

That name brought a spark of animation—and fury—to her face. "I've *no* interest in hearing about him," she said coldly.

"I know," he said quickly. Ned was his cousin's child, a fatherless boy who'd been often at Anandale as a child.

Anthony's father was a cold and rather heartless fellow, so Anthony had also come to Anandale at times. Patrick had thought they'd been like brothers.

The previous summer, though, Ned had destroyed that belief. Deeply in debt, he'd set his cap for winning Celia, then a wealthy widow. When she fell in love with Anthony instead, Ned had not taken it well. He'd tried to disrupt their engagement by telling lies about Anthony, and had even pointed a pistol at Celia in an attempt to hold her for ransom.

Patrick had shot him then. Not fatally—Ned could no longer lift his arm over his head, but he was alive. Patrick gave him the choice of Australia or America over facing the magistrate in England, on the condition he never return. Ned had chosen Virginia, and sailed with his arm still bandaged in a sling.

"No, it's not directly about him. It's about his mother, Janet."

Her rigid posture did not change, and she yanked on the threads with enough force to snap them.

Patrick forged on. "Janet—Nettie is my cousin, you might know. She's never been a steady woman, and this business with Ned... It didn't help." That was the kindest way to put it. Nettie had become deranged, in Patrick's opinion. "She was not pleased with me for banishing Ned."

"Even after what he did?" Rosalind gave him a cool glare.

"Oh, she didn't believe a word of that." He sighed, fingering a teal colored skein. "She never could believe Ned to be at fault for anything, and I never confronted her about it —foolishly, I see now. Her husband deserted her, leaving her with a young boy and no income. I took pity on her then, but I admit, I should have said more to open her eyes.

"She was waiting when I returned to Anandale this summer, and carried on like a banshee, wailing that she'd been betrayed, that I had stolen her child from her, that her death would be upon my head..." He grimaced, remembering the full force of Nettie's wild fury.

"Indeed."

"I felt sorry for her," he admitted. "'Tis a hard thing to hear of your only child. I once loved the boy like my own son! But what he did was unpardonable. It was for her sake I let him go to Virginia, but she saw only that I made him go, not that he should have gone to prison instead."

"Lord Warfield, this really does not concern me. Are those all the green flosses?"

He looked down at his handful of little balls of thread. "Aye."

"Thank you, sir." She took them and brought out a needle and some kind of embroidery.

"Nettie stole the letters," he said. Rosalind looked up in surprise. "Mine to you, and some of yours to me. I thought you'd stopped writing. I thought you no longer cared." He fiddled uncomfortably with his hands, now empty. "I still wrote to you, but she was very underhanded and she stole them from my secretary's desk."

For a moment she sat unmoving, then gave herself a shake. "Well. That was very wrong of her, but what's done is done."

Oh Lord. She'd lost all affection for him. "I didn't know she'd done it until a few weeks ago—"

"You stayed in Scotland," she interrupted. "When you left you said you would be back by the end of summer, but you stayed months longer."

"Nettie," he said in growing urgency. "She's lost her reason. She—she started a fire that near burned down my stable. She fed sand into a batch of whiskey and ruined it all. She poisoned my housekeeper, and I had to pension off the poor woman and hire a new one. I was running mad, from one mishap to the next, tearing out my hair trying to sort who was behind it."

Rosalind was staring at him in mingled shock and disbelief, but before she could speak, Anthony and Celia returned, flush with love for their baby, who had indeed been sound asleep. They described at great length how adorably he slept in his cot, and Patrick could only smile and nod even as his heart felt like lead in his chest.

On impulse he excused himself and went to his room. If she'd set her mind against him, it would be easy for her to dismiss, but he had nothing to lose now. He went back to the drawing room, where Celia was sitting at the pianoforte, laughing, and Anthony was holding up pages of music, teasing her about which one she should play.

Patrick's heart twisted at the sight of the love they shared. He thought he'd been on the brink of the same himself, and now he feared it would all come to naught. At the age of fifty, the odds of falling in love with a different woman were slim. It had seemed like a bloody miracle when he met Rosalind and felt that odd sort of silly happiness poets described, for the first and only time in his life.

Rosalind was smiling at the musical antics as she stitched. Patrick paused in front of her and bowed. "Here," he said gruffly. "'Tis all I can offer in testimony to what I told you." He held out the packet, and, looking startled, she took it.

He went over to the pianoforte and chased away his nephew. Would Rosalind read the letters, all those letters he'd written to her since the summer? Would it change her feelings, to see how puzzled and then worried he'd become at the absence of replies from her? Would she forgive him for being such a stupid idiot not to catch on that Nettie, with her wild accusations and crying fits, had been so determined to punish him that she stole what he valued most?

No, he didn't want to see if she read the letters or threw them on the fire. Instead he sang while Celia played, eventually allowing Anthony to join him. The fire crackled, the air was scented with greenery brought in, and occasionally the snow blew hard and furious against the windowpanes.

And all Patrick could see was Rosalind, barely visible from the corner of his eye, her sewing put aside and his letters in her hand.

She read them. All of them, from what he could tell. But she didn't look at him or speak to him the rest of the evening.

He wondered what she was thinking. He himself had been shocked when he discovered them in Nettie's sewing basket, some with needles stuck through, some with childish scrawls of ink across them. His secretary had muttered about papers being mislaid for some time, but MacLeish was getting rather old now, and Patrick had been too distracted by the fire and spoilt batch of whiskey, his prized estate product, to do more than tell him to take more care where he put things. Only when poor Mrs. Carrigan had fallen seriously ill, and told him that she suspected Nettie of putting henbane in her soup, had Patrick finally seen the truth. His cousin had gone mad in her grief and turned on him.

That was a failing of his, he acknowledged. Just as he hadn't believed Ned capable of any serious harm, he'd never thought Nettie, who had been his childhood playmate, could nurture such hatred and spite that she tried to kill a woman.

When the singing was done and the fire had died down, everyone said good night and retired. Patrick paced his room, wondering if he should try to speak to Rosalind or wait for her to approach him. It would be dashed awkward to live in the same house with her for the next three weeks without clearing the air, and then he thought he should just go back to Anandale if she had no interest in clearing the air.

But no; he would not admit defeat until she told him definitively. He must wait a few days, for the sake of a peaceful holiday, and then he'd ask, simply and directly, and see.

A knock at the door startled him. When he opened it, Rosalind stood there, the packet of letters in her hand. "What did you do?"

He tensed. "What do you mean?"

She held up the packet. "When you realized she'd taken these, and done... all the rest."

"I sent her to Virginia, to be with her son." He heaved a

sigh. "We played together as children. She's gone mad, I'm sure of it, but I couldn't put her in an asylum. Perhaps with Ned, she'll be restored. Perhaps they'll both be restored to sense. Once, they were dear to me, and I hope some shadow of those creatures still lives inside them."

Slowly she nodded. "There are seventeen letters here."

He had written to her at least once a fortnight, even when he thought she'd stopped replying, describing the chaos at his estate, explaining reasons for his delay in returning to London, asking increasingly worried queries about her regard for him.

"She filched all but the last one." He peered at her closely. "Did you read the last one?"

Color rose in her cheeks. "I did."

"And did you like it?" He all but held his breath. The last one was an anguished excoriation of himself, for being blind to Nettie and to Ned, for having let so much time slip by without suspecting the truth. It ended with a vow to explain himself if she ever granted him the chance. He'd written it the day before Anthony's invitation arrived, and then decided to deliver it himself.

Rosalind tilted her head, nibbling her lip. "It was a start." She put out her hand. "Perhaps you'll come tell me more."

"Everything," he said fervently, closing his door behind him and taking her hand, to follow her into her sitting room across the corridor.

## 3

Rosalind sat bolt upright with a start, her heart racing. The room was dark, the fire died down to coals, and for a moment she simply sat, frozen with alarm and uncertainty.

There was a stirring beside her. "Is aught amiss?" whispered a gravelly voice she knew so well.

He was here. Her pulse calmed a bit. He should *not* be here, of course, in her room, on her bed, but for a moment, she'd feared that the whole prior evening had not happened.

They had sat in her sitting room talking until the small hours of the morning. As shocking as the story had first seemed to her, Rosalind knew he was not a liar.

Nor had his interest in her ever wavered. Those seventeen letters had unfolded his constancy and determination to care for his estate, then his struggle to find a compassionate solution for his deranged cousin. Each one had ended with his hope that he would soon be free to return to England and see her.

And Rosalind had fallen headfirst back into that charmed state, just listening to his voice and watching the way his face changed as he spoke. When she'd been unable to keep her eyes open, he'd walked her to the bed and given her the sweetest kiss goodnight...

"You're still here," she whispered in relief. "Patrick—"

"You're beautiful when you sleep." His fingers grazed her cheek. "I only meant to look on you for a minute, and then another, and then I fell asleep myself."

"That's how it always is with you," she said, but smiling. "One minute, then one more, then another, and before I know it you've wormed your way in and I can't get rid of you."

"Persistence is my only virtue." With a rustle, he got off the bed and made his way across the room. She heard the flint strike, and the glow of a candle illuminated his face.

Like herself, he was fully dressed. His cravat was askew, and his ginger hair was ruffled on one side of his head, but when he grinned hopefully at her, she couldn't help but smile back. She swung her feet over the side of the bed, only then realizing that he'd draped a blanket over her. No wonder she'd slept so long. "Never again shall I stay up so late."

"Fear not, lass. If ever you did, I'd carry you to bed and tuck you up safe." He came over and put the candle down on the table near the bed. "If you'd want me to, that is."

Reluctantly she smiled. "Who else would?"

"Whoever did would be the luckiest bloke in the whole of Britain." He went down on one knee and took her hand, holding her fingers lightly. "I still hope to be that lucky bloke, you know."

She couldn't imagine it being anyone else. "You're a devil, Patrick Murray, a silver-tongued devil who manages to tempt me into throwing away my good sense."

He brightened and slipped his free hand into the pocket of his waistcoat. "That's encouraging. Can I tempt you into saying yes once more?" He held up a ring. The candlelight made the sapphire glow.

Rosalind looked at it, then at him. "Have you had that in your pocket all night?"

"No," he said. "It's been in my pocket since July, waiting only for a chance to offer it to you."

She blinked. "July…"

"Why'd I go all the way back to Anandale? I had to fetch it. All the Warfield brides have worn this sapphire. My grandmother took it from my grandfather and wore it thirty-seven years. Then my mam wore it the next forty-two. " He tilted her hand back and forth, studying her fingers. "I hope you'll wear it for the next thirty years at least."

"Is that a marriage proposal?" she asked in a daze. Of all the times she'd pictured receiving one from him, it had never been like this.

"Of course it is," he said a bit acerbically. "I don't go about giving jewels to any woman who strolls by, not even for Christmas. Only you, lass." He grinned up at her, endearingly abashed. "Will you have me, Rosalind? To have and to hold, to love and to scold? For I do love you, lass. Might have done since the day I met you."

She took the ring and held it up. "You'd better not run off to Scotland without me again."

He scoffed. "I've no interest in leaving you. If you put that ring on your finger, you shall have my loyalty, and my honesty, for all time. Even if I must write letters every day to prove it."

"Letters?" She did like the ring. It was beautiful, and she found it very touching that it had been his mother's and grandmother's. "Where will you go that you'll need to write letters?"

"I suppose I'll have to go back to my room before morning, to avoid causing a scene." He grinned. "I could write the first one there, as a gift. It's Christmas morn now."

Rosalind raised one brow. "A letter from across the hall!"

"I can compose it now." He cleared his throat. "My darling duchess. I love you. I love you madly. Marry me, please. Your devoted servant, Warfield."

She slid the ring on her finger to see how it looked. "I suppose you'd have to bribe a footman to deliver it."

"No doubt." He tilted his head, grinning hopefully. "Will you keep wearing the ring?"

Rosalind pursed her lips. "Yes, Lord Warfield, I think I shall."

His eyes grew brighter. "And…?"

"Yes, Patrick," she amended. "I will marry you." And she leaned forward, cupping his handsome face in her hands, and kissed him. "For I do love you, too."

———

R ead Anthony's and Celia's story in **A Rake's Guide to Seduction.**

# GRACE'S CHRISTMAS HERO

*Every year, Grace Finch hopes to sit near her childhood friend Oliver Ford at Christmas dinner. Every year she falls a little more in love with him. But will Oliver ever feel the same for her?*

1802

Grace Finch first met Oliver Ford at a party at her aunt's house. Aunt Sarah had invited the Fords because Mrs. Ford had recently passed away, and it was the father and son's first Christmas without her. They were neighbors, although distant ones.

Despite being reserved, Oliver was quickly absorbed into the group of children, who were bent on playing hide and seek in the elaborate gardens behind Holkham House, now glittering with a crust of snow, before darkness fell and they would be sent to the nursery for dinner.

"What are you doing, Gracie?" asked her older sister Daphne in amusement as Grace struggled with her boots.

"Going out to play in the gardens, with you."

Daphne laughed. "Of course not! You're too little. You must be at least seven to go outside."

Grace's eyes went wide. She was six, and had been counting the days until this party. "I am not! I'm going, Daphne, I am!"

Still laughing, Daphne only shook her head and went out with their cousins Lizzie and Frederick. They were all eleven, five years older than Grace, who could only watch impotently. She couldn't manage her boots alone yet. Amelia,

James, and George were already outside, running and shouting in delight as they threw snow at each other. It would be such fun, and a tear slipped down her cheek at the thought of missing it all, stuck in the house with babies like her sister Willa, who was only two.

"Here," said a kind boy's voice. Oliver knelt at her feet and tied first one, then the other bootlace. "Now you can go out," he whispered, his blue eyes shining at her from under his untidy mop of blond hair. He even winked at her.

"Thank you." Grace beamed at him, and ran into the garden.

Lizzie won the game, but Grace remembered the kindness.

## 1808

When she was twelve, Grace's mother said she could sit at the lower table at Aunt Sarah's, with the other cousins who were too old for the nursery but not yet adults. Nervous but eager, Grace chose her best dress and brushed her hair one hundred careful strokes. She promised to bring Willa a cracker from the table and went down to eat, hoping she wasn't seated next to Frederick, who liked to tease.

Oliver Ford was there, down from Oxford, tall and lanky at age seventeen. He and his father were regulars at Christmas dinner now. He wasn't the most talkative boy, but he still had a friendly grin and an easy laugh, and Amelia and Daphne seemed to find him far more interesting than ever before. Grace watched her sister and cousin monopolize his attention with a frown. She wanted to talk to him, too. Oliver always talked to her, year after year. He never put snow down her neck or pulled her hair when her braids fell down, like Frederick did.

But her hopes were rewarded when a last-minute ruckus ended with him and Frederick changing seats, putting Oliver beside her. "Happy Christmas, Oliver," she wished him shyly as the servants brought out the roast.

"And to you, Miss Grace." His blue eyes shone. "All grown up now!"

She laughed, pleased. "Not really. Not like you." She glanced at her sister and cousin, who looked annoyed. Frederick was between them now, and he was being obnoxious, tossing spoons back and forth across the table with James in spite of his mother's commands to stop. "But more than Frederick," she couldn't resist adding.

Oliver grinned. "You're far more mature than Frederick." His voice was deeper this year, she realized. It suited him.

"Everyone is," she told him, earning a laugh.

They talked the rest of the meal. It was her favorite Christmas dinner ever.

War made Christmas somber.

Frederick was serving as a ensign under General Wellington in Portugal. James had been pleading to buy a commission for a year, and Grace's father had finally agreed to it; James would be off in the spring to fight Napoleon. Oliver was a lieutenant in the Royal Navy, patrolling the waters in far-off Scandinavia.

All the adults spoke anxiously of places like Salamanca and Borodino, and three young men from their small village in Hertfordshire had been killed this year alone. This year so many family members were gone, Aunt Sarah set up only one table, which was bittersweet to Grace.

But as the roasted goose was brought out, there was a loud knock on the door. Everyone fell silent—it was ominous, that knocking—and Uncle Daniel leapt from his chair to follow the butler. He returned quickly, his face wreathed in smiles. "Look who washed ashore," he cried, and to Grace's shocked delight, Oliver stepped into the room.

Everyone rushed to embrace him, Mr. Ford leading the way. "Only a short furlough," Oliver explained as everyone wanted to shake his hand. "I must return in a week."

"Then you must make the most of it!" exclaimed Aunt

Sarah. "Come, we've only just sat down to dinner." She motioned to the servants to shift the places around the table.

"Oh, no, just squeeze me in on an empty corner, Lady Holkham," Oliver told her.

And quite without thinking, Grace blurted out, "There's room next to my place."

Oliver's blue eyes swung to her and lit up, almost as if he'd been searching for her among the crowd. "Perfect," he said. "Put me there. By Grace."

She hid her blush by rushing to help lay the place. "Thank you," he whispered as he took the seat beside her. "If I happen to yawn, please don't tell anyone."

"Of course not. How long was your journey?" It felt unspeakably special to share this private conversation with him, while everyone in the room was anxious to hear what had happened to him in the Navy and how he thought the war was going.

"Two days. My captain's family is conveniently near, at Deal." He grinned. "And it's that to which I owe this furlough. I understand his wife is due to have a baby within the month and he was desperate for any excuse to come ashore for a few days."

Grace smiled. "And much joy to them, since they've caused so much here! It's wonderful to have you home, Oliver."

"It's wonderful to be home." He ducked his head even nearer hers. "And to see you, Grace."

It was hard to contain the explosion of joy this statement caused inside her. With great effort she kept her poise and listened raptly as he answered everyone's questions about the Navy. But their hands brushed when she passed him the sauce boat, and he smiled at her with particular warmth, and it set her heart soaring and whirling in her chest.

After dinner, Aunt Sarah called for dancing. "We must make a little merrier this year," she declared. "To send James on his way, and to celebrate Oliver's brief return."

The furniture was moved aside in the drawing room and Grace's mother sat at the pianoforte to play. Willa bounced to the center of the room, pulling James with her, and Lizzie and Amelia both looked expectantly at Oliver, tall and handsome in his uniform.

But he turned to Grace. "May I have the first set?" he asked.

"Of—of course," she stammered.

They danced more than once, as it happened. This evening no mother protested that it was growing late, and by the time the candles began to gutter out, even Grace's feet hurt. She sat on the sofa and discreetly toed off her slippers.

Oliver sat with a thump beside her. "It's good to be home," he declared, "but it's also tiring!"

Grace, who had never left home as he had done, smiled. "I'm glad you're here to be tired out dancing with all of us."

He turned to her. "So am I." He hesitated, then laid his hand right next to hers, so their fingers just touched. "I have to leave in a few days. Grace… would you write to me?"

The air in the room seemed to rush out, leaving her light-headed and gasping. "Yes," she managed to reply, "of course."

His hand covered hers, only for a moment. "Thank you."

She wet her lips. His fingers were still touching hers, Oliver's fingers, so much larger and stronger than her own. His one hand could cover both of hers. "Is it very lonely out on the ocean?"

"It is." His mouth turned up on one side. "We might go months without sight of anything familiar, but when we get supplies and letters from home… It makes any day a good day."

"I'll write every week," she promised.

He laughed. "I won't get letters that often! But Grace…" He angled himself toward her, a great beaming grin on his face. "If you did, I'd treasure every one."

## 1816

The war was over, and this year everyone seemed certain it would stay over.

James came home with a scar on his face and a Waterloo medal. Grace had never seen her mother weep so loudly as the day he rode his horse back up the drive to their sprawling house.

Grace's sisters had both married, and she and Willa were the only ones left at home. Amelia had married Squire Bennet's son on the other side of Rochester, and they came to Aunt Sarah's Christmas dinner still. Daphne lived in London, now Lady Cartwright, and she had promised Willa a season in town next year when she was seventeen. Willa, slender and beautiful, was alive with excitement. Grace, shorter and not so slender, was quiet with envy.

She had gone to London, not for a whole Season but for a long visit to her Aunt Mary. Even though she loved it there— the museums, the concerts, the glorious theater!—she had not 'taken' in the way girls needed to take to be sent for a whole season.

Willa, on the other hand, was vivacious and pretty and everyone agreed she could make a splendid match if given the opportunity. Grace would stay home with her books and her animals and her sketch books, while Willa would have a new wardrobe and go to London in the spring.

As if that weren't enough to put a damper on Christmas, Oliver didn't come. He wrote to her still, but he'd been very vague about why he wouldn't be at Holkham House this year as usual. Quite aside from the fact that she was now twenty and feeling very conscious of her unmarried state, she missed him. He hadn't been to Canterbury in months.

"He's in the Admiralty now, not free to gallivant about the country," said Mr. Ford proudly when she asked how Oliver was. "Quite invaluable to his superiors, you know." He chuckled. "And I might as well tell you—there's a pretty commodore's daughter who might have helped keep him in Portsmouth."

Grace's mouth hung open for a full minute. "Oh," she said stupidly. "I did not know. He didn't mention her in his letters…"

Mr. Ford's smile turned gentle, as if he suspected her heart had just suffered a blow. "I understand she's a lively one. He appears quite dazzled, but it may come to nothing."

"Perhaps," she said numbly.

"And there," Mr. Ford went on in his bracing but kind way. "He'll be a sorry lad when I tell him you asked about him. Always very fond of you, Miss Finch—one year he told me he wouldn't come unless I promised you would be here. He said you were the only interesting person to talk to."

She'd tried to be interesting. She wrote to him about the birds she saw and drew in her sketchbook, of the lame rabbit she saved from a poacher and kept as a pet. She sent him a letter every week, as she'd promised years ago. But she wasn't a pretty commodore's daughter, and Oliver hadn't been home in a year.

There wasn't much that was happy about this Christmas.

G race did not want to go to Christmas dinner at her Aunt Sarah's house anymore.

As of the previous September, she was the only unmarried cousin of the lot. Daphne, with her baronet husband, had two little boys, and Lizzie had a daughter. Her sister Amelia had four children now, who ran in the Holkham garden as Grace used to do with her cousins. James, George, Willa... Even Frederick had found someone to marry.

She wasn't unmarried for lack of offers. She'd had two— well, one reasonable offer and one that might be counted as a mercy proposal. No one had expected her to accept that, although her papa had told her he would have consented, if she'd wanted to marry the fellow.

Her mother had been hopeful about the other one, though. His family had a very handsome property near Rochester. "You'd be but thirty miles from home, dear," she'd told Grace hopefully.

But Grace thought she'd rather be a spinster forever than marry Donald Brewster. He was polite but dull, and she'd never really wanted to marry someone as short as she was. Their children would be elves, she thought morosely. She'd always dreamed of someone tall... kind and friendly... even handsome, with sun-bleached blond hair and bright blue eyes...

All right, she'd dreamed of Oliver. Since the day he tied her bootlaces so many years ago. She had expected her infatuation would fade and be supplanted by some other attraction, but it never had, no matter how desperately she had tried after hearing about the commodore's daughter in Portsmouth.

Oliver hadn't married that girl, though, and he'd kept writing to Grace, and somehow her heart never gave up hope.

She told herself that was enough; she was perfectly contented and resigned to being unmarried, trading letters every few weeks with the man of her dreams, even if he would never know how much she cared for him. She'd even created her own sort of employment. Two years ago she had begun selling her drawings of various animals and plants around her family home, and a professor from Oxford had come down to talk to her about illustrating his treatise on the flora and fauna of Kent after discovering her engravings in a print shop. She was not useless, even if her father described her new work as "drawing grasshoppers and daisies." The professor was paying her, and if it went well, she might become one of those independent women with their own income and their own cottages with a cat in the window. She would be avant-garde, rather than sad and forlorn.

Still, she didn't look forward to dinner at Holkham House.

She walked in the door, resigned to being Aunt Grace, who could always be counted on to hold someone's baby because she had none of her own. Perhaps this year she'd start drinking when Uncle Daniel brought out his raisin-wine.

But that idea blew away like the fat flakes of snow flurrying down outside when Oliver Ford stepped out of the drawing room.

Her heart seized. Her feet stopped. She hadn't seen him in over a year, and he was even more handsome now than ever. He was still in the Navy, and his uniform was spotless, the braid glinting in the candlelight.

"Grace." He bowed, an uncertain smile on his face. "I hoped you would come."

She tried to shake off her grim mood. "*I* always come," she reminded him lightly. "I didn't expect to see *you*!" She went to meet him, hands outstretched. As always, a little charge shot up her arms as his fingers clasped hers.

"I had to invite myself," he confided. "Lady Holkham's invitation was addressed to my father."

She laughed. "I'm sure Aunt Sarah was delighted to add you to the party." She knew her aunt had invited him every year in the hope he might marry one of her cousins. Grace had overheard Mother tell Papa that Oliver made a tidy fortune in the war. But now all the cousins were married, so that didn't matter.

"I suspect I threw off her numbers," he murmured. He was still holding her hands, and now he stepped back to gaze at her. "You look splendid."

She smiled brightly even as his blue eyes made her heart twist. "Thank you. I'm trying to *be* splendid."

He grinned. "Ah, I've known you're splendid all along."

Grace tensed—what did that mean?—but he only dropped her hand and went to greet her parents. She watched him speak to her father, and tried not to sigh. She almost wished he *would* get married so she could stop hoping. Every time she set eyes on his strong profile, his tanned face, even the way he stood, something inside her grew warm and soft. Hopeful.

He came back to her after a while. "Are you anxious to see your cousins and aunt and uncle?"

Good heavens; did he know she hadn't wanted to come? "I see them frequently," she said with a forced laugh. "Lizzie's boy is getting quite tall, isn't he?"

Oliver didn't laugh. He watched her closely, as if studying her face. Grace fell silent, nervous now. She cleared her throat. "Why do you ask?"

"Because," he answered slowly, "I was hoping you might agree to take a walk with me in the garden."

She blinked. "It's snowing."

"I won't put it down your collar." He winked. "I want to talk to you."

He knew all about the professor from Oxford and the sketches of grasshoppers and daisies. She'd written to him almost before she'd told her parents. She wrote to tell him about everything that happened to her here in this quiet little corner of Kent.

"Talk to me about what?" she asked stupidly.

He looked sheepish. "About… something important."

Dread clutched at her. "Are you getting married?" she blurted out in a whisper.

Oliver went still. He was, she knew it. Grace tried to pull free—when had he got hold of her hand again?—but he wouldn't let go.

"Congratulations," she said, her voice wobbly.

Oliver cursed under his breath and turned on his heel, towing her behind him out the door, through the arbor, into the garden. There he faced her. "We've known each other a long time." He waited for her wary nod of agreement. "I think we've been very good friends for at least a dozen years now."

Again Grace nodded.

Oliver drew a deep breath. "I have never looked forward to anything like I do to your letters, Grace. I feel like I know you, and you know me, better than anyone in the world, even my father."

The snow picked up, and plenty of snowflakes hit her bare nape. But somehow Grace wasn't cold as Oliver, dear Oliver, her closest confidant, the object of all her romantic dreams and wishes, reached for her hand again. "I've been away in Portsmouth a long time, and I have to go back in a fortnight. But while I'm here, I would like to see you." She gasped. That dangerous, tempting grin curved his mouth. "I would like to call on you. Your father gave me his permission."

"That's what you wanted to talk to me about?"

He glanced at the house, then stepped closer. He leaned down until she could see every tiny fleck of gray in his blue eyes. Almost forehead to forehead, he gazed into her eyes. "No. I wanted to ask you to marry me, but your parents—"

She flung her arms around him and kissed him. Oliver's arms closed around her and he lifted her off her feet, kissing her back. When he finally lifted his head, Grace's brain could only form one thought. "My parents don't want me to marry you?"

He laughed. "Your father said I should call first, so we could be re-acquainted."

She laughed, too. "But we already are." She cupped his cheek with one cold hand. "You were right—we *do* know each other better than anyone else. My answer is yes."

"To which question?"

She smiled, her heart bursting. "To *all* of them."

And when he kissed her again, she didn't even feel the snow.

# A KISS FOR CHRISTMAS

*Thomas Weston is dumbstruck at the sight of Miss Clara Hampton.
Unfortunately she's nearly engaged to another man... unless
Thomas can win her heart.*
*A* Scandals *Story*

SOMERSETSHIRE 1790

It was agreed by everyone in Wells that Miss Clara Hampton would marry Mr. Johnathan Mortimer, son and heir of Sir Eliot Mortimer.

After all, it was the ideal match; Mr. Mortimer was the most eligible catch within twenty miles, and Miss Hampton was the acknowledged beauty of that same realm. He was rich and she was beautiful, and what could be more perfect?

Clara herself was in favor of this arrangement. Her father didn't have the wealth to sponsor a trip to London, and unlike Agnes Wilson she had no aunt in town who could invite her to visit. Clara had always known she must find someone close to home. Mr. Mortimer was thoroughly respectable, and given the dearth of men with expectations—let alone attractive ones with some wit and charm—he was the best possible choice.

The man himself also seemed amenable to the idea. For all of last winter and spring he had smiled at Clara, and made a point of seeking out her company at parties. He danced with her regularly and even called once at Hampton Close, although some unkind gossips pointed out that he had called on Mr. Hampton, and not Miss Hampton at all.

Clara didn't mind that. She knew that Mr. Mortimer had contrived to take a turn in the garden with her before seeing her father, and he had been as admiring as could be.

All was proceeding splendidly…until it was not.

Mr. Mortimer went away in the summer, as young men often did, to London and then to Bath. But he did not come home until late in the fall, and when he did, it soon became clear things were not the same.

Mr. Mortimer kept to his male friends; he only rarely came to assemblies and no longer danced with anyone, including Clara. He didn't come to call. Mrs. Hampton turned to her network of gossipy friends for intelligence, but no one had heard anything out of the ordinary. Mr. Mortimer might have had some high times in town, Mrs. Hampton assured her daughter, but he was home now, and would settle down soon.

But the days passed and he did not.

After three weeks of neglect, Clara's patience ran out. She was soon to be twenty-three, and had thought herself almost engaged. They had laughed together and he had kissed her fingers and called her his dear. She was not about to sit back and allow some other girl to attach him. This year, this Christmas, she would fix Mr. Mortimer's interest for good.

"Someone is watching you, Clara," teased Meredith Holliwell, in the middle of the winter ball at the assembly rooms.

"Oh?" She smiled in pleasure. "Who is it?"

"The tall gentleman over there," said her cousin, giving her fan a swish in the direction. "*Not* Mr. Mortimer."

Clara hid her disappointment. She angled her head, trying to spy out who it was without turning around and attracting any notice in doing so. Merry had gestured at a cluster of gentlemen at the other end of the room. One was Johnathan Mortimer, who was—alas—not looking her way at all. Another, Mr. Hodge, was short, and one of the taller ones had his back to her.

There was no doubt whom Merry meant. It was the last member of the group, a stranger she didn't recognize. He was tall, about Mr. Mortimer's height, with dark hair and broad shoulders. His clothing was every bit as fine as Mr. Mortimer's, and he stood with easy grace, as if he were the equal of every man present

The trouble, though, was that since he was already looking at her, he noticed her spying immediately. And as soon as her gaze met his, the scoundrel grinned.

Clara gave him a reproving little frown and turned her back. "Impertinent fellow," she whispered to Merry.

Her cousin's eyebrows went up. "How could you tell?"

"He was staring at me and then he grinned."

Merry heaved a sigh. "Oh, the agonies you suffer, Clara. I don't know how you endure."

"It was an impertinent grin," she added.

Merry darted a glance over her shoulder, toward the gentleman in question. "Too bad," she murmured. "He's rather handsome."

"Not as handsome as John Mortimer." Clara wasn't about to be distracted by a stranger.

"True, but we can't all marry Sir Eliot's son," Merry pointed out philosophically. "I wonder who the other fellow is."

"I've no idea. Perhaps Lydia knows."

Lydia Pitt, two years older and married, was already coming to join them. "I'm so glad you both came tonight," she said warmly. "I've been reduced to sitting with the dowagers, for want of someone to talk to!"

"Dowagers!" Clara smiled. "If you sit with them, it's only because they know the best gossip."

"They do," said Lydia without a blink. "But I'd rather dance most nights."

"Speaking of gossip," said Merry, "do you know who the tall fellow with the auburn hair is?" She motioned discreetly with her fan again. "The one staring at Clara."

"Merry!" said Clara in censure, but Lydia boldly looked.

"Oh, yes. His name is Weston. He's an attorney, in practice with his father in Kent. I've seen him in town for the last few days. I think he's employed by Sir Eliot Mortimer."

That caused an uncomfortable flurry in Clara's breast. How awkward it would be if he was at Mortimer Lodge when she and Mama called. Her mother had agreed with her that it was time to make a bold strike, and they had planned to visit Lady Mortimer.

Hopefully that man was a little tipsy tonight and would remember his manners in the morning, or better yet, forget entirely that she'd caught him staring at her.

"An attorney!" Merry was disappointed. "He looks too elegant to be an attorney."

"Well." Lydia lowered her voice. "Rumor is he's a well-off attorney. Mrs. Smythe took the effort to find out all she could —she has three daughters, one can hardly blame her for noticing a handsome gentleman new to town—and she decided his fortune was plump enough to overshadow his profession."

Merry and Clara exchanged a glance, Merry's speculative and Clara's surprised. That must be a very plump fortune, if Mrs. Smythe was blinded by it. She was a viscount's grand-daughter and had lofty ambitions for her three girls.

"What sort of fellow is he?"

"Merry," Clara said in shock.

Her cousin widened her eyes. "What? I didn't ask for an introduction, only gossip."

Lydia laughed. "Gossip is all I have! I've never met the man. But David has, and he said Mr. Weston is ambitious and canny. Intelligent," she added. "Rather a clever lawyer, too."

"Handsome, clever, and rich." Merry looked pleased. "Perhaps an introduction wouldn't be unpleasant."

"Did you say he was staring at Clara?" Lydia glanced toward him again.

"Yes, but only because she was standing in front of *me*, I believe."

Clara had to laugh at Merry's outrageous statement, and she was laughing still when a voice spoke behind her. "I beg your pardon, miss, but did you drop this handkerchief?"

## ❧ 2 ❧

Thomas Weston was a betting man. And tonight he was about to make a bet he had every hope of losing.

It took some effort. His tendency to win had made people leery of accepting his bets. That was unfortunate, as Thomas liked a good wager. Even more he liked to win, but John Mortimer had already declared he wouldn't stake a penny against anything Thomas wanted.

"The devil's own luck," Mortimer called it, with a laugh that wasn't entirely good-natured, and all his friends rushed to follow suit.

Thomas knew it wasn't entirely luck. He never placed a wager without doing a fair bit of calculation, research, and outright snooping, in some cases. The greater the amount at stake, the more careful he was to weigh how much he wanted it, how likely he was to get it, and how he could shift the odds in his favor before he put his money at risk. If none of the other gentlemen put in the effort, they had only themselves to blame when they lost.

Tonight a prize had caught his eye, though, that he knew hit all the wrong marks. His desire had struck him like a thunderbolt, sudden and intense, blowing away any thought of calculation, let alone the opportunity for research. While he wanted it very much, he was quite certain his chances were virtually nil at the moment. Therefore that meant he had to do something drastic to better his odds.

Snooping and conniving were his only options.

"I say, Mortimer," he said to the young gentleman beside him. "You were having me on all this time."

"Eh?" Mortimer was surreptitiously sipping brandy from a flask he kept sliding out of his tail pocket. "About what?"

Thomas gave him a severe look. "This assembly! You told me Wells was the most pitiable backwater, without a thing of interest about it and no society, either. But there are some uncommonly pretty girls here tonight."

Mortimer's face went blank for a moment, then relaxed into his usual exaggerated ennui. "Well, *you* may think so! There are some pretty enough, I suppose, to someone of your background."

Mortimer fancied himself a gentleman of the ton, after his summer in London. Thomas, who had been going to London regularly for years now, kept quiet about it.

"Yes," he said aloud. "To someone of my background—and eyesight—there are some lovely creatures here."

Jenkins, one of Mortimer's mates, snickered. "Handsome they may be, but none of 'em are eligible enough for Mortimer." The man himself tilted his head slightly, tacitly agreeing with this nonsense.

"Eligible!" Thomas laughed. "Any one of you lot would be fortunate to get a dance with one of those ladies over there." He nodded across the room.

Jenkins scoffed. "Dance! We could get a *dance*—especially Morty. Every single woman in this room is wasting away for a smile from him."

"Who wants to dance with a girl who's got no money, though?" put in Hodge. "Morty's got the right idea."

"That the only thing to commend a lady is her fortune?"

Thomas glanced with interest at Mortimer, whose neck was red above his collar. "Is that it, Mortimer?"

"Shut it, Hodge. You'll give Weston the wrong idea." Mortimer looked surly as he drank from his flask.

"You see, Weston," drawled Jenkins patronizingly, "in the better circles, it doesn't *do* to encourage a poor girl to get the wrong idea. If Morty danced with any of them, they'd start planning a wedding, when he means no such thing."

"Huh." Thomas sipped his wine, weak and watered though it was. "Not even that one?"

Hodge swung around to see who his deliberately vague comment could refer to.

"Only one is worthwhile," said Jenkins with a snicker.

Almost there. "The one in green?"

"No, the one—" Mortimer motioned with one hand, forgetting he held his flask and sloshing brandy over his cuff. "The one in purple."

*Now* Thomas could look at her, and he did so, striving hard to keep his expression placid. It was harder than it should have been. She was the loveliest female he had ever set eyes on. Her dark gold hair was piled up in fashionable curls, and her mulberry gown showed off a trim waist and very handsome bosom. Her dress was fashionable but relatively unadorned, and the only jewelry she wore was a simple locket around her neck. A gentleman's daughter but no heiress, he guessed, a girl with aspirations based more on her pretty face than her family and fortune.

Thomas could afford to overlook the lack of dowry. In fact, he would have overlooked a towering debt, at least for tonight. Hers was a *very* pretty face.

As he was watching, she peeked over her shoulder at him. A gentleman would have looked away immediately, affecting that he hadn't been staring her way. Thomas grinned instead. He couldn't help it. Her dark eyes—grey? Perhaps blue?— widened, and a charming frown pinched her brow before she pointedly turned her back to him.

"Miss Clara Hampton," supplied Jenkins. "Fetching little thing, ain't she? Never said we didn't have *any* pretty girls here in Wells."

"But she's only got eyes for Morty," added Hodge.

Thomas turned to his scowling host in pretend astonishment. "Has she! Mortimer, you fortunate fellow. She's lovely."

"I suppose she is," agreed Mortimer reluctantly, after a pause.

"Regrettably she's got no dowry," put in Jenkins.

"That's why she's sighing after Morty," said Hodge with a smirk. "Biggest estate in the parish, and all that." He glanced at Thomas. "Thought you'd have twigged to that, as his attorney."

Thomas just smiled. What he knew was that the Mortimer family was in a spot of financial trouble they were very keen to keep quiet. That was why they had hired him, a stranger to the county, instead of their usual solicitor. Mortimer was keeping his head down because he was the party at fault; it was his gambling that had entangled his family with unpleasant people, and it was his father who had put Thomas in charge of his affairs until, as the elder Mortimer acidly put it, "this nightmare is behind us."

Hence Thomas's invitation to this gathering. Part of his duties included keeping Mortimer from the card tables, which neither of them were enjoying. Still, Thomas hadn't appreciated until now that it might come with some benefits.

"That isn't why," snapped Mortimer, glaring at his half-drunk friend.

"Well, it's part of it," protested Hodge. "Ain't that why all the girls stare and sigh when you walk by? They'd all like to be a baronetess."

Mortimer's frown deepened peevishly. "Be quiet, Hodge. It's not a matter of wealth, or beauty. I shan't marry that young lady because she's... Well, she's too provincial for me, you know."

Thomas raised his brows as the other men hooted and

laughed. Mortimer smiled, smug again, and drank more of his brandy, his swagger restored.

Thomas was not surprised. Mortimer thought himself far, far above this small town now, with his six months of town bronze and rakish behavior, even if he was forced to keep the latter quiet.

"No one now will do for our Mr. Mortimer but the finest lady in London," cried Hodge, sweeping an unsteady bow. "None of these country girls for him!"

"Suit yourself." Thomas shrugged.

"Weston thinks you're mad, Morty," teased Jenkins. "Overlooking little Miss Hampton for a London lady with ten thousand pounds!"

Thomas smiled, knowing there was no London lady with ten thousand pounds waiting to accept Mortimer's proposal. "Not all of us can be so confident."

"*You* should dance with her, Weston," slurred Hodge. "She needs a rich husband, now that Mortimer's decided against her."

Mortimer scowled, jerking upright at this suggestion that Thomas might step into his place with a woman, even a woman he had just declared himself wholly disinterested in.

"Ten pounds she'd laugh in my face," said Thomas swiftly. "Such a young lady, dance with me, especially when she'd set her heart on someone like Mortimer? I've got no estate at all, and she just gave me a ferocious frown."

Hodge guffawed, and Jenkins grinned, an evil light in his eye.

"No bet," muttered Mortimer.

"Twenty pounds says she will!" declared Hodge, listing off balance as he poked Thomas in the shoulder. He either hadn't heard Mortimer or was too drunk to care. "The Hamptons have nothing, I daresay you'd be good enough for them."

Thomas hesitated a heartbeat, just long to make it look good, then nodded. "Done."

"No bet," snarled Mortimer suddenly.

A hush descended. His friends, while not knowing the true depths of Mortimer's embarrassment, were aware that he was in his father's black books over some wagers gone bad.

On the one hand, Mortimer had been belligerently claiming all evening that he wasn't about to get caught and leg-shackled by any of the hopeful misses here tonight. On the other, he was well accustomed to being the focus of every female eye in the room, and even if he denied it, Mortimer liked being wanted, even by those he disdained.

"Eh? What's that? Thought you didn't want her, Morty," said Hodge—helpfully, to Thomas's cause.

"Thank you, Mortimer. How touching to know you think she'd gladly take my hand," said Thomas with a mock bow.

He only provoked the man because he knew Sir Eliot Mortimer was actively searching for a bride with a healthy dowry for his son, and Hodge had already said Miss Hampton didn't have one. He only risked it because he knew Sir Eliot had declared Mortimer would not wed at all without his permission, if he wanted to maintain his inheritance and allowance. He only dared because he knew who Mortimer really fancied, and it wasn't anybody in this room.

And blessedly, Mortimer obliged him. "Never said that," he snapped. "She hasn't got a farthing, so I suppose if you want to dance with her, the joke's on you. I just think even she has higher standards than an *attorney*."

His mates cackled with laughter as Mortimer looked smug.

Thomas lifted one shoulder, trying to hide his bubbling elation. "We'll find out." And he strolled off to lose twenty pounds.

If there were anything worse than not being asked to dance by the man on one's desire, it must be a request for a dance from the *wrong* man. And even worse, he did so with a purely transparent ploy.

Clara gave the bold stranger a cool glance when he interrupted their group. Did he think her simple-minded? Pretending she'd dropped her handkerchief, as a pretext to solicit an introduction! "No, sir, I did not."

"Er…" said Merry quietly. "I think you did, Clara. It's got your monogram."

Clara blinked, and looked at the handkerchief in the man's hand for the first time. Her face grew warm as she realized her cousin was correct; there was a small C embroidered in the corner of the handkerchief. "Oh—that is—yes, actually, perhaps I did. Thank you, sir."

He smiled very easily. "It is a lovely handkerchief, I would not wish it to be lost." He bowed. "Thomas Weston, at your service, ladies."

All three of them curtsied, and Lydia bravely introduced herself and the rest of them. Merry was studying him with open interest and Lydia, as usual, was not deterred by having no acquaintance to speak of.

"How do you do, sir?" she asked warmly. "I think you may be acquainted with my husband, Mr. David Pitt."

"I am indeed!" His eyes lit up and he made another tiny bow to Lydia. "A marvelous fellow he is. I am delighted to make your acquaintance as well, Mrs. Pitt."

Lydia blushed and preened. "You are new to town, are you not, sir?"

"I am." He shot a rueful look at Merry. "So new I have not been introduced to any ladies who might like to dance."

Merry laughed. "Now you have been! Clara, weren't you expressing a desire to dance?"

Clara glared at her cousin, who knew perfectly well that she had been scheming to dance with Mr. Mortimer, and calculating how she would engineer it.

Mr. Weston turned to her, his expression hopeful. "Miss Hampton, perhaps you would honor me with a set?"

John Mortimer remained stubbornly at the far side of the room, barricaded behind his idle friends, but he *was* watching her. Perhaps if he saw her dancing with someone else, he would be spurred to action. *A little jealousy might inspire the man,* Mama had suggested just the other night.

And she *had* been wrong about the handkerchief.

So she smiled at Mr. Weston and offered her hand. "The pleasure would be mine, Mr. Weston." And she walked out with him for the quadrille.

Now, of course, she had to talk to him. "You're not from Somerset," she said as they formed the set with three other couples.

"No, from Kent." He gave her a funny little smile, somehow enticing and self-deprecating at once. "Far from home, alone in a strange land…"

Clara choked on a giggle. "Not so strange, sir."

She dared a glance toward Mr. Mortimer. He was watching her, his head angled as if puzzled. Perhaps Mama was right about jealousy—not that Clara meant to *flirt* with Mr. Weston. She felt she and Mr. Mortimer had had an understanding, and she was loyal and true. Still, she gave Mr. Weston a warm smile.

"I feel like a stranger," he confessed. "What are the sights to see in Wells? Perhaps I will feel more at home if I make myself familiar with the country."

"There is the cathedral, of course, and the Bishop's Palace." Then Clara stopped, because there was precious little else to excite anyone's interest in Wells.

"I have been to both, and enjoyed them immensely, if not entirely devoutly," he said as they joined hands. "What else?"

"I suggest a trip to Bath," she said. "If you wish to see anything else of note."

He looked at her a moment too long, his blue eyes openly admiring. "I have already seen more beauty in Wells than I ever saw in Bath."

She blushed in spite of herself as the dance sent them apart. It was cheeky, but she wasn't immune to a compliment from a handsome man. "If the weather were fair, I would suggest an expedition to the Roman ruins nearby."

"It is a bit cold for that," he agreed, looking a little downcast.

Clara bit her lip in chagrin that Wells was so small and provincial. "'Tis the Christmas season," she offered. "There will be parties, I'm sure."

"Yes." Now he was embarrassed. Too late Clara realized that, as a stranger to town, he wasn't likely to be invited to the usual parties, unless Mr. Mortimer brought him along. Oh, how could she have been so stupid?

"My mother is planning a small evening party, two weeks from this Friday," she heard herself say. "We would be delighted to have you join us."

His face changed, subtly but undeniably. Anyone watching wouldn't have known, but Clara could tell by his eyes he was elated. "Thank you, Miss Hampton," he said, his voice warm and low. "I would like that about all things."

She was still wracking her brain for how to tell her mother

what she'd done when Mr. Weston escorted her back to her friends. Mama had planned the Christmas party as the perfect opportunity for Mr. Mortimer to remember Clara's charms—if necessary by having them thrust into his face. There were innumerable games young people could play at Christmastide that would give her ample opportunity to speak with Mr. Mortimer and re-acquaint him with how charming, pleasant, and marriageable Clara was.

And now Clara herself, despite having her hopes pinned on just that, had gone and invited another man.

A handsome other man.

A *rich* other man.

She found her mother and confessed at once. To her astonishment, Mama was pleased. "Well done," was her response.

"What?" Clara blinked and lowered her voice. "Truly, Mama? I thought Mr. Mortimer—"

"Yes, yes." Mama patted her hand. "I asked your father, and he tells me Mr. Weston is an eligible man in his own right. Not a baronet's heir, of course, but Papa heard he made a handsome sum investing in coal canals. Mr. Delahunt was decidedly impressed by him, and spoke very highly of his intelligence and sense. And though he is only an attorney, Sir Eliot Mortimer did summon him all the way from Kent, which is noteworthy indeed."

"So you're pleased to have Mr. Weston?" Clara asked, nonplussed.

"Yes, of course, dear! We'll keep your sights on Mr. Mortimer, naturally, but there is Helen to think of, or even Merry."

For some reason it did not sit entirely well with Clara that Mama was so eager to throw Mr. Weston to her younger sister or to her cousin. Particularly not when Merry had already spoken so approvingly of his looks and danced with him after Clara had.

She glanced back at Mr. Weston. He was just beginning a set with Patience Shaw, who was smiling up at him with a great deal of interest. Patience was a year older than Clara, and Mama said her parents were growing anxious for her to marry—anxious enough that they deigned to allow Mr. Bates's youngest son William call on her. Mr. Weston would be a decided improvement on young Mr. Bates, for Patience.

Well. Clara turned her back to him. Handsome he might be, and rich as well, but he was not John Mortimer, who had been the object of her interest for two years now. She was not going to allow herself to be distracted by dancing blue eyes and a teasing smile or even by fine dancing.

But it did not help that across the room, Mr. Mortimer sulked and drank and refused to dance a single set with anyone, especially Clara.

※ 4 ※

**J**ohn Mortimer was not pleased when Thomas mentioned the Hamptons' party.

"You're going?" he demanded. "Why would you?"

Thomas quirked a brow. "I was invited by Miss Hampton."

Mortimer scowled. They both knew Thomas would have gone if Mortimer did, at his father's orders. But the fact that Thomas had a right to attend independently clearly rankled.

"A dull country party," Mortimer finally said. "Snapdragon and whist and blindman's bluff. Children's games."

"Jolly good fun on a winter's evening," rejoined Thomas.

Mortimer rolled his eyes. "Would that we could go to Bath."

Thomas said nothing. Bath was where Mortimer had got himself in trouble, and had been explicitly commanded to avoid.

"I wasn't even planning to attend," complained Mortimer.

"I am perfectly capable of attending alone, if you wish to remain at the Lodge."

Mortimer almost growled at him in disgust. His father had decreed that he could not go out unless Thomas went with him, not to the tavern, not to the assembly rooms, and not to Bath under any circumstances. He was only permitted to make calls on family friends by himself—one of the last things Mortimer wished to do—or attend church—the very last thing he wished to do—without Thomas.

It put John Mortimer in a dreadful mood, and he took it out on Thomas. Since Sir Eliot had warned him it might go this way, and offered extremely handsome compensation in anticipation of it, Thomas absorbed Mortimer's bad temper with a shrug and good humor.

"It won't be very amusing," Mortimer finally said. "You'll regret it."

"And yet I intend to go anyway, having been duly apprised of that."

"You're supposed to go where *I* go."

Thomas raised his brows. "And where do you intend to go, a fortnight from Friday?"

Mortimer grumbled and complained, but in the end admitted he probably would have gone to the Hamptons' party. "So I suppose you'll have to go, too," he finished, as if the conversation hadn't begun by Thomas remarking that he meant to go anyway.

"I suppose I shall," he agreed, and kept his smile on the inside.


C lara was not surprised to encounter Mr. Weston several times in the next fortnight.

That was due to Wells, of course. In a small town with no attractions of note, it was inevitable that they would cross paths at church or at the shops. And it should have been offset by the fact that every time she met Mr. Weston, he was in company with Mr. Mortimer, and Mr. Weston's friendly greetings meant that Mr. Mortimer also spoke to her repeatedly.

And yet it was not.

The first time it was easy to excuse. She and her sister met both gentlemen outside the bookseller's. It was only polite to talk with them for several minutes.

The second time they were lingering outside the bakery, savoring the aroma, when the gentlemen happened by, apparently with the same idea. They stood and talked for quite a while about which bread was the most delicious.

The third time it was rainy, and when Clara dropped her umbrella, Mr. Weston appeared almost out of nowhere with another. Mr. Mortimer took it from him and guided her to the tea shop where her cousin and aunt were waiting, and then the gentlemen joined them for tea.

But after three such meetings, she could not lie to herself any longer. It might not be a surprise to encounter him, but Clara *was* surprised at how quickly she came to look forward to meeting Mr. Weston.

Mr. Mortimer spoke to her, too, but not the way he had in the spring. He told her about his new hunter, how much more pleasant Bath was than Wells, and how the spate of cold weather made it dashed dreary and cast him into the doldrums. Clara listened politely, but never once did he ask about her opinion, her thoughts, her family.

Sometimes she suspected the only reason he spoke to her at all was to Mr. Weston from doing it. It was as clear as day to Clara, who had two younger brothers, that Mr. Mortimer was determined not to give way to Mr. Weston.

Mr. Weston, on the other hand, asked after her cousin and her friend Lydia, if they were not with Clara. He made her laugh with his wry comments in response to Mr. Mortimer's —there was no other word for it—sulkiness. His smile was genuine, and his compliments felt honest as well. She found herself smiling whenever they parted, even if they'd only exchanged a few words.

"I cede all interest in Mr. Mortimer to you," remarked Merry after they had met him and Mr. Mortimer in High Street one day.

"Merry," sighed Clara. "Please don't."

"What? You think I ought to set my cap for Johnathan Mortimer, too?"

"Don't be silly."

"Well, I wouldn't want him," her cousin went on. "So morose! I wonder what has happened. He used to be charming—at least, more charming than this."

Clara had been having the same unkind thought. Mr. Mortimer had used to seem pleased to see her, with a smile and a warm greeting. He used to ask after her family, and make easy conversation that wasn't strictly about him. Now she had the awkward feeling that his sole purpose in speaking to her was to prevent Mr. Weston from capturing her interest.

Clara didn't know what to think of Mr. Weston. He was friendly and amusing but he was only in town for a short time. She liked meeting him very much, but he'd given no indication he meant anything other than a brief friendship.

"Perhaps Mama knows," she said to her cousin. "I suppose your mother has heard nothing?"

Merry made a face. Aunt Willa was passionate about botany and horticulture and cared nothing at all for the newest fashions in bonnets or how best to flirt during the quadrille, topics Merry could and would discuss endlessly. "She was mildly interested to hear a gentleman of some manners and good fortune will be at your mother's Christmas party. *Another chance, dear,* she said."

Clara bit her lip. It was wrong of her to be so focused on her own travails when Merry was just as unwed and suitor-less as she was. "He seems very pleased to attend," she offered. "It is a good chance to make his acquaintance."

Merry gave her a look, half exasperated, half mischievous. "It's *your* acquaintance he wants to make, Clara."

She blushed. "The party is at my home, that's all…"

Merry snorted. "You're being ridiculous! And what's more…" She stopped walking, forcing Clara to a stop, too.

"You're being willfully blind. Mr. Weston is intrigued by you, and Mr. Mortimer is not."

Clara stared at her, sure in her heart that Merry was right. "Why?" she asked in despair. "He was so solicitous earlier this year!"

"That was months ago," Merry pointed out—rather callously, to Clara's ears.

"But it is so much more *sensible* for me to marry Mr. Mortimer," she argued, though without passion.

"So you can stay in Wells forever, dancing with the same twenty gentlemen at the same assembly rooms and gossiping with the same ladies you've known all your life?" Merry heaved a dramatic sigh. "I would throw myself at the first gentleman with five hundred a year who swore to carry me away from Somerset entirely."

Clara frowned in affront. "I would never throw myself at a man."

"Clara." Merry pressed her hand. "You don't have to. And while I will admit Mr. Mortimer is the most eligible man in Wells... that only means Wells is tragically bereft of eligible men."

Clara walked home, troubled. She could not deny that Mr. Weston was more engaging and charming than Mr. Mortimer was now—perhaps than he'd ever been. He was at least as handsome, too, although he had an air of slightly naughty humor about him, which was unlike Mr. Mortimer.

Unfortunately she found that indecently appealing.

But Johnathan Mortimer was familiar; her family knew his family. He was handsome and would have a very pretty estate. She had fixed her hopes on him because... because...

She couldn't remember. Had it been her mother's idea, perhaps? It had seemed so logical and yet now Clara couldn't precisely recall why she'd ever wanted him.

Well. She would try to view both gentlemen fairly at the party in two days, and see what her feelings were after that. What more could she do?

## 5

The evening of the Hamptons' party was cold and clear, with the scent of snow in the air.

Thomas whistled softly as he dressed, looking forward to the evening with more eagerness than any man ought to admit. He'd met Miss Hampton nearly a dozen times in the last fortnight, and each encounter only served to make him more captivated. She was even lovelier close up, with sparkling dark blue eyes and a pretty pink in her cheeks. She laughed easily and smiled even more. If she crooked her finger at him this evening, Thomas thought he'd knock people over in his haste to get to her side.

By the time he had moved on to contemplating, with extreme pleasure, dancing with her again, his manservant, Mack, ducked into the room, closing the door behind him. "From Mr. Harker," he reported, holding out a sealed note.

Well, damn. The one thing that could ruin this evening. Thomas abandoned his neckcloth and tore open the note.

He read it, sighed, and threw the paper on the bureau.

"Trouble, sir?" asked Mack, holding up his coat without being asked.

Thomas slid in his arms and jerked the coat into place.

Mack, who was far more secretary than valet, gave the sleeves a cursory flick with the brush. "Mary Anne Carlow."

"Ah." Mick grimaced. "What does Mr. Harker suggest?"

Thomas didn't reply for a moment, his thoughts racing. Mary Anne Carlow was the reason he was here in Wells, the reason John Mortimer was in his father's black books. She was tall and beautiful and quite possibly a scheming minx, with her crystal blue eyes fixed on Mortimer's handsome expectations. It was to her brother and his friends that Mortimer had gambled away an outrageous sum of money, and Thomas thought that was no coincidence.

In Mortimer's telling, it was all a matter between friends, nothing to get upset about. He had met James Pettison and his mates at the Royal Academy, and they hit it off immediately, attending the theater, riding in Hype Park, and savoring the delights of Vauxhall.

Thomas heard that Mortimer had also gone to brothels and gaming hells and notorious private clubs. After thoroughly exposing Mortimer to the wicked side of London, Pettison declared himself bored in London and proposed they go to Bath, where his sister lived.

Mrs. Mary Anne Carlow was, to put it simply, the sort of woman men made fools of themselves over. Seductive and worldly, with a throaty laugh and a forthright manner, Mortimer had been bowled over. He admitted he'd shared her bed, but protested that they were in love and engaged to marry.

That, most likely, was the part that had enraged Sir Eliot the most. Losing six thousand pounds to Pettison and his ominous mates was bad enough, but wanting to marry an adventuress put the baronet's nose well out of joint.

Thomas thought the whole thing was a trap laid for a brash young idiot. Mortimer refused to consider any such possibility. He was sure Pettison had played fairly, and he was certain that Mrs. Carlow was desperately in love with him.

"Harker suspects Mrs. Carlow has been in contact with Mortimer. Have you seen any sign of it? Suspicious letters, messengers sneaking in and out?" he asked Mack.

His man frowned. "No, but I'll ask the other servants."

"Do that." Thomas finished tying his neckcloth. All the Mortimers would be with him tonight at the Hamptons' Christmas party, where neither Pettison nor Mrs. Carlow could sneak in without being seen. He wasn't going to let Mortimer's foolishness spoil this evening for him.

He hoped.

Clara walked through the house, straightening greenery and shuffling the sheet music. Guests were to arrive soon, and she was having trouble sitting still.

Mama had smiled knowingly at her restlessness and murmured something about Mr. Mortimer. Clara had not corrected her, that she was not thinking of Mr. Mortimer, but of the London attorney who shadowed Mr. Mortimer's footsteps and thoroughly outshone the man she'd once expected to marry.

Two years ago, it had been entirely reasonable to dream of John Mortimer. She certainly hadn't been the only girl in Wells who did. And for a few months last spring, he had acted as if he returned her interest. No, he'd never declared himself, but his behavior had made the whole town think he *would*. If not for the recent turn of events, Clara would be highly annoyed at Mr. Mortimer for that.

But now… it seemed she had changed her mind about him, just as he'd changed his mind about her.

When the guests began arriving, she greeted everyone with a warm smile. Merry came first, with her parents and two brothers, then Lydia and her husband, followed quickly by the Shaws, the Delahunts, the Cartwrights, the Smythes, the Hodges, and her Aunt and Uncle Radcliffe. The older people were directed to the dining room, where her mother had laid out the best wines and cordials, while the young people were sent to the drawing room. Everyone would dine together, but Papa had declared he had no stomach for an evening of games and dancing, and Mama had obliged him by setting up a card room away from the drawing room.

The Mortimer party arrived nearly last, with Mr. Weston bringing up the rear. Mama whispered to Helen while Papa was greeting Sir Eliot and Lady Mortimer, and Clara watched her sister curtsy to Mr. Weston and welcome him to Hampton Close. He answered her pleasantly, but when he looked up and caught Clara's eye, his face lit up and he smiled.

Her heart did a funny little double thump in her chest. She smiled back, but inside felt a leaping sort of excitement that boded well for the evening.

Everyone was in good spirits. They ate a buffet supper with plum cakes and mince pies, and sang carols. There was a little bit of dancing, but Aunt Radcliffe, on the harpsichord, claimed tired fingers after an hour, and Amelia Hodge, the next best musician, didn't wish to play. The older adults soon withdrew to the card room and the small parlor Mama had set aside for those who disdained cards, and Arthur closed the drawing room door for the games.

They played move-all, where there was always one less chair than people needing a place to sit, to cries of outrage and amusement. Even Mr. Mortimer was in better spirits than he had been lately. Clara didn't care, and took it only as yet another sign the man was fickle. They played charades, in which Sylvia Smythe had to portray the burning of Rome and nearly caught her dress on fire. They played Buffy in the Shade, where Clara's brother George guessed that Patience Shaw must be their cousin William, and received a ferocious glare in return. George was still apologizing when Lydia clapped her hands and called for quiet.

"The next game will be familiar to everyone, and yet not," she cried. "You all know hide and seek—"

"Oh yes!" cried Caroline Delahunt, barely sixteen and joining the young people for the first time this year.

"But in reverse," finished Lydia with a twinkle in her eye. "One person will hide, and all the rest will seek!"

A murmur of confusion rumbled over them. Clara glanced toward Mr. Weston. He had been enjoying himself, laughing and talking with everyone, but not once had he sought her out. He'd stuck fairly close to Mr. Mortimer, despite the occasional irritated glances from that gentleman.

She wished he'd made more of an effort to speak to her. During charades she had maneuvered to sit beside him, and although he'd been cordial, there had been nothing particularly warm in his attention.

Clara was puzzled—and exasperated. What was wrong? Why did gentleman start to pay her attention, then immediately lose interest the moment she decided she liked them? Did that mean their interest wasn't real, or was *she* less interesting than they'd thought?

"Now," Lydia continued, "once someone discovers the one who has hidden, he must join them in hiding. So must the next person to discover them, and so on until there is only one person left seeking. That person will win the dunce prize, which is to be the accused in our next game, The Prisoner." Groans greeted this, and George called out that he would just hide himself if he were last. "No, you won't, George Hampton, for we shall find you," Lydia told him.

She had collected a handful of straws and now broke one in half, before circulating through the crowd until everyone had drawn one. Clara realized at once that hers was the broken one, and Lydia beamed at her. "Clara, you must hide! Take care to choose a place that will hold at least fifteen."

"But there are eighteen of us," protested Patience.

"Then I s'pose we'll have to crowd in together," drawled John Hodge. The gentlemen looked more intrigued at this news.

Clara handed the straw back to Lydia. "How much time have I got?"

"To a count of fifty."

"Right." She gave a cheery curtsy as everyone called out encouragement. She avoided looking at Mr. Weston. "See you all soon!"

## ❦  6  ❦

Thomas was not enjoying the evening nearly as much as he'd hoped to.

He had been obliged to report Harker's news to Sir Eliot, who'd turned the color of turnips. His wife had prevailed upon him not to harangue their son this evening, but in consequence Sir Eliot had ordered Thomas to stay right by his side all evening.

To make it all worse, Mortimer was in high spirits this evening, much jollier than he'd been in weeks. It made Thomas suspect Harker was correct, and Mrs. Carlow had managed to contact him. Like that, his hope of catching Miss Hampton in a private moment was snuffed out. He didn't even dare dance with her, because he could barely look away from her even when he *wasn't* supposed to be attending to her as a dance partner.

Instead he must make sure Mortimer had no chance of slipping out, or communicating with anyone outside the guests. Thomas had no idea how Sir Eliot thought this would happen, but it was the baronet's explicit order, and since the baronet was here, mere yards away, Thomas knew he was trapped.

To console himself he danced with Helen Hampton. "I

hear you're in love with my sister," were her first words to him.

He grinned. "Who told you that?"

"My cousin, Merry," she said as they clasped hands and turned.

"Ah." He stole a glance at Clara, partnered with Frederick Delahunt. "I do admire Miss Hampton very much."

"Well, if you want a chance, you had better seize the moment," she told him. "Clara's been in love with Mr. Mortimer for a year or more."

"I see," he managed to say. He hadn't thought her feelings were that deep. "Does he return her regard?"

"This spring we thought so," she told him frankly. "Everyone was sure he would propose. He's been rather distant since he returned, but my sister is good at getting what she wants. I suppose if she wants him back, she'll find a way. Unless you persuade her otherwise, that is."

Sobered, Thomas went through the steps of the dance. Knowing what he did, he hated to think of any young woman pining over John Mortimer. And yet, he thought Clara Hampton was intelligent and sensible, and Mortimer had given absolutely no encouragement to her or anyone in Wells nursing romantic dreams of him. Surely she must know.

It only made him resent Mortimer more, Mortimer who was laughing with John Hodge and Arthur Hampton and having a splendid time while Thomas was forced to watch over him like a nursemaid.

And then Clara drew the short straw to start the hide-and-seek, and Thomas realized his opportunities were running out. He sidled up to George Hampton, still chastened from his misadventures in Buffy in the Shade, and whispered a few questions.

Snooping and conniving were always useful options.

· · ·

C lara debated where to hide. Obviously she could not go to the dining room, where the servants were still clearing away the supper, or the morning room or parlor, where her parents and their guests were. Where else? Hampton Close was an old house, a rambling warren of small rooms and winding passages, but she had no wish to be stuck in some of them for as long as this might take…

She darted up the stairs and raced down the corridor. There was a large room at the head of the stairs. Family lore held that one day some forty years ago, the Prince of Wales had passed through town while out riding with his entourage. In the heat of the day, they had stopped and asked for refreshment, which Clara's grandfather provided with alacrity. Though they stayed barely an hour, and only an over-heated retainer had actually entered the house and rested in the room, it was henceforth called, wryly, the Royal Apartment.

Now it was where the family gathered in the evenings, with a harp for Helen to play and comfortable chairs around the large hearth. But there was also a closet at the back. It was too small and dark for any use other than storage, but Clara thought fifteen people could fit, if they stood very still.

She heard the sounds of people downstairs beginning to seek, and hurried to the closet. The hinges creaked faintly as she opened it, but the closet was warm, thanks to the flues behind it. She closed the door softly, and settled in to wait.

She almost hoped no one would find her. It was warm and restful here in the closet, and she was suddenly tired of the Christmas party. Far from fixing Mr. Mortimer's interest, as Mama had hoped, Clara couldn't wait for him—and his attorney—to go home. She was done with the both of them. Perhaps it was time to embrace spinsterhood and persuade Merry they ought to set up house together, very economically, in Bath, and go to the assembly rooms and dance all night.

She leaned against the wall, trying not to think about Mr. Weston. She'd known him a few weeks, not nearly long enough to get her heart broken. Still, she'd genuinely liked him. Even when she'd thought her destiny was another man, she had looked forward to seeing *him* and talking to him. Better to learn now that he was just as fickle as Mr. Mortimer, of course, but still… she couldn't stop wishing he'd been more heroic.

Sunk in her thoughts, she almost missed the soft whisper as the closet door creaked. "Miss Hampton?"

Clara revived herself. "Yes," she whispered back. Silly game. What had got into Lydia, suggesting this?

The person came in, his entrance announced more by the rush of cooler air than by any flood of light. The room beyond was nearly as dark as the closet. Clara shifted to allow the newcomer to find his bearings in the pitch-dark space. She could tell it was a man, but nothing more.

"Thank goodness you chose a warm hiding spot," he whispered. "Some fellows were talking of the attics."

Now she recognized the voice. "We should be very quiet, Mr. Weston," she whispered back.

"Right, right." She heard him moving his feet. "Although, isn't the point to be found?"

Clara sighed. Now that her moment of solitude was gone, it was. "I suppose."

There was a moment of silence. "Thank you for inviting me tonight," he said.

"You are welcome, sir."

"Your brothers are quite the scamps," he went on, in the same hushed whisper. "I like them."

Clara's temper simmered. "Lovely," she muttered.

"George told me he wants to ride horses at Astley's," the oblivious man went on. "I wish I'd had that sort of nerve when I was his age."

Clara said nothing.

"And your sister is marvelous," he said. Clara's mood grew darker; she had noted that he danced with Helen when he didn't ask *her* for a set. "Very high spirited and—"

"We're supposed to be quiet," she said shortly.

He was, for a long moment. "Miss Hampton, I fear I have offended you."

"How could you have," she said before she could stop herself, "when we've not exchanged ten words all evening?"

"That was not my choice."

Clara rolled her eyes. "I have long noticed, Mr. Weston, that when a man truly wishes to do something, he generally manages to do it."

"Right," he said, noticeably chagrined. "Will you allow me to explain?"

"Why do you need to explain? I do not feel owed your conversation."

"Of course not. I—" He exhaled. "Yes of course. You're right. I could have spoken to you, and I did not, and I am very sorry for it."

Clara sniffed. "Then why didn't you?" She shouldn't care but she couldn't stop herself from asking.

"I felt obliged to attend to… other things."

"If you were obliged elsewhere, and fulfilled that obligation, then you have nothing to regret."

"But I didn't want to be," he said quickly. "It was not more pleasant—indeed, nothing is more pleasant than talking to you—"

"Not even dancing with my sister?"

"Er—that was delightful, but…" He cleared his throat. "I would have preferred to dance with *you*. You had already given your hand to Mr. Delahunt."

"I suppose you should ask more quickly next time," she said, again before she could think better of it.

"You give no quarter, do you?" he asked, rueful and admiring at once.

"Quarter? For what reason? You said you wished to speak to me, but you did not. You said you wished to dance with me, but you did not ask. Mr. Weston, as far as I can see, you are your own obstacle."

Finally he laughed, quietly. "And I fancy myself an attorney! I confess: I am completely at fault."

Clara felt a glow of satisfaction at this admission, even though it hardly improved things. "Now that we are in agreement, we can continue being quiet and wait to be discovered by the rest of the party." Not that she was anxious for that. Even arguing with him was more exhilarating than expected. This was what she had hoped for with Mr. Weston, even if she might have wished for a happier topic.

"How shall I make amends, though?"

"You assume I am injured by this behavior."

"It put you out of temper," he pointed out.

Clara scoffed. "You pretending a lack of control over your own actions put me out of temper, sir."

"Touché," he murmured. "Then how shall I make it up to you?"

She should have said it was immaterial to her, but instead what came out of her mouth was, "Why are you in Wells?"

"Ah," he said softly. "The lady plays hard."

"You don't have to answer, of course. I had already decided you aren't worth any anguish."

"No, wait," he said at once. "Sir Eliot engaged me on a legal matter."

"Yes, Mr. Weston, we all know that. No one thought you came to Wells for a holiday," she said witheringly.

He was quiet for a moment. "Mr. John Mortimer encountered some… difficulties and I am here to help him. I cannot say more."

"All right," she said after a moment.

"I am fiendishly glad I did, too, for I would never have met you otherwise. Even when every other aspect of my time here grows enormously frustrating, I am still fervently glad I took the position."

Her temper was being rapidly appeased. "And what shall happen when your employment with Sir Eliot ends? I suppose you've got a family, friends, a home, perhaps a dog waiting for you back in Kent."

He laughed. "I haven't got a dog, or a home. My family is already used to my being gone for long stretches. But as for what happens when I've concluded my work for Sir Eliot... That depends."

Instinctively she knew he meant her—it depended on *her*. A flush of warmth stole over her, not simply pleasure at the flattery but a deeper, more potent happiness.

"I wonder why it's taking everyone so long to discover us," she said to keep herself, this once, from speaking too freely.

"Oh. Yes, that. I might have an idea..."

"What?" Clara asked with a laugh, at his sheepish tone. "I thought it was a good hiding spot, but far from the best. George ought to have guessed it by now."

"I might, perhaps, have closed the door behind me when I came into the room out there."

Clara's mouth fell open. "You locked me in here? With you?"

"I did not lock it," he said swiftly. "You were—and are—free to go at any time. I merely closed the door."

"How did you even know I was hiding in here?"

"The scent of your perfume," he said. "A sense that you had come this way. The yearning of my own heart, following you." Clara rolled her eyes, even as she smiled, at this blatant but flattering foolishness. "And... I might have bribed your brother George to tell me the most likely place to find you, and to lead everyone else in the opposite direction."

She blinked, then burst into a smothered fit of laughter. "That's cheating!"

"All's fair," he said with a small laugh of his own, "in love and Christmas games."

"Love," she repeated.

"Miss Hampton." He was right beside her; she could tell from his voice and the faint scent of his shaving soap, an unfamiliar smell that made her want to inhale deeply, to know that one little thing about him. Her skirt stirred, and then his fingers brushed her wrist. "I think it might be."

She let him hold her hand. "What would decide the matter?"

"You," he said simply.

"I hardly know what to answer," she whispered as he raised her hand to his mouth.

"Then don't answer, not yet. I would like to call on you. Dance with you. Walk up and down the absurdly short row of shops in High Street with you." She laughed. His lips brushed her wrist and a shiver went through her. "Allow me to demonstrate that I am not, in fact, the feckless idiot I've acted tonight."

"I suppose that would be all right," she said breathlessly as the door behind them creaked open.

"Clara?" whispered George loudly.

"Yes," she hissed. Beside her, Mr. Weston lowered her hand, but didn't release it. He kept holding it, and she let him, as first George, then Merry, and then more and more people crowded in, until she and Mr. Weston were pressed against the back wall, with Arthur's elbow in her stomach and Patience Shaw muttering anxiously about dark closed spaces.

"Thank you," he breathed by her ear.

For reply she turned her hand in his and threaded her fingers through his. They stayed that way until finally Amelia Hodge, the last seeker, threw open the door and declared it a very silly game, and that she was ready to play so they could dance again.

This time, Clara danced twice with Mr. Weston, who didn't hesitate a moment to ask. And she barely even noticed who John Mortimer danced with at all.

## 7

Thomas awoke three days later, on Christmas morning, to the sounds of Sir Eliot shouting.

The baronet was in a fine fury; Mortimer Lodge was a solid house, heavily built of brick. But sound had a way of traveling from the wide front hall up the stairs, and Thomas supposed the entire household could hear him railing away at some poor soul.

It didn't occur to him that it might affect *him* until Mack banged down his door and burst in. "John Mortimer's run off," he said in a frantic whisper.

Thomas sat up and then leapt from bed. "What?"

"Sir Eliot intercepted Mr. Harker's man from Bath and badgered it out of him." Mack stepped forward and held out a crumpled note. "He managed to get me this before Sir Eliot came down."

Thomas ripped it open and read it in a moment. "Damn," he said softly. "Harker says Mrs. Carlow has been shopping lavishly and hinting that she plans to be married soon. And at dawn this morning she got into a travel chaise with a man who looks very like John Mortimer." He looked up. "I suppose Sir Eliot has verified that his son is not here."

Mack nodded. "Near whipped the footman up the stairs to look."

"Well, that tears it." Sir Eliot would rage at him for letting John Mortimer slip the net, even though his son had been at dinner the previous evening and stayed up playing cards until midnight with his parents and sisters. John was clearly wilier than his father gave him credit for. He must have run for it soon after the household went to bed, to have been in Bath before dawn. The fact that he'd slipped out of his family home instead of the assembly rooms would not spare Thomas from Sir Eliot's fury, though.

"So... what?" asked Mack uncertainly.

Thomas huffed in mirthless laugher. "I'll be sacked."

Mack shuffled his feet. "Does... does that matter much, sir?"

He made a face and flicked away the question. No, it did not matter, except that he wanted to stay in Wells now... he did not want to be sent on his way... he wanted to see more of Clara Hampton and her sparkling eyes and her clever mouth...

"Good God," he breathed as realization hit him. Clara. Everyone in Wells still thought she was hoping to marry John Mortimer, and even though Thomas knew she was not—he was *sure* she was not—she shouldn't be caught off guard by the news that Mortimer had eloped with another woman.

"Send for a horse," he told Mack, striding to the wardrobe and rifling inside for clothes. "I have to go out."

"Right, sir." Mack ducked out and Thomas dressed quickly.

He dodged Sir Eliot, who was still bellowing at his wife in the morning parlor, quietly lifted his coat from the back stairs, and took off for Hampton Close. If John Mortimer had left late last night, it was unlikely anyone there would have heard of it yet. That wouldn't take long, though, the way Sir Eliot was carrying on; gossip seemed to travel faster than any horse in small towns.

He rode up the winding drive of Hampton Close, the house so still and comfortable and... quiet. For the first time Thomas thought to check his watch.

Good Lord. It was earlier than he'd thought. And it was Christmas morning, when the family might not welcome him barging in.

And what would Miss Hampton think of him, rushing to tell her this? What if her feelings for John Mortimer were deeper than he thought? What if his coming to tell her the news was mortifying? Perhaps he ought to have sent a letter, so she could absorb the news in privacy and compose herself...

He might have convinced himself to go back—it was rather cold out and he'd forgotten his gloves in his haste—if the door hadn't opened a few minutes later, and the lady he'd wanted to see slipped out.

"Mr. Weston?" she called quizzically. "Are you well?"

With a start he jumped off the horse. "No. That is, yes, I'm perfectly well, but I've just realized it's much too early to knock on the door—"

"Fortunately for you, I saw you from the window." She pulled a green shawl around her shoulders against the frigid air. She wore a dress of scarlet and yellow, and a smile so brilliant and warm it almost knocked him over. "What brought you here, so early you didn't wish to knock?"

He grimaced at his own stupidity. "I had news I wished to tell you, before anyone else could..." He hesitated, then knotted the horse's reins and let him go. He offered her his arm.

Clara took it, perplexed. He looked anxious and uneasy. When she'd spotted him through the window on the stairs, her heart had soared. Why could he possibly have come to see her, first thing on Christmas morning, but to declare himself? She had flung a shawl over herself and run outside to see, ignoring her sister's calls to come to breakfast.

But perhaps that had been wrong. Perhaps Mr. Weston

had come to tell her he was leaving Wells. He'd told David Pitt he would, when his employment with Sir Eliot ended.

"Is it good news or bad?" she asked before he could begin.

He cut a worrisome glance at her. "I don't know."

Clara pulled her shawl tighter around her. "Then I think you'd better just say it."

"Right." He blew out his breath in a frosty puff. "Mr. John Mortimer has, it appears, left town." He paused. "And he may possibly have eloped with a woman in Bath."

Clara pondered that. "I see what you mean," she murmured. "Is that good, or bad? On the one hand, if he cares for her and she for him, it could be very happy. But on the other hand, eloping suggests there is something disreputable about the liaison. It could go either way, I'm afraid. Have you come seeking my opinion on the question? I'm as in the dark as you seem to be, I'm afraid."

He cleared his throat but it sounded like a laugh. "No. I wanted to be sure you knew before someone had a chance to spring it on you unawares."

"Ah, I see. You feared my heart would be broken."

His arm twitched under her hand, and he avoided her gaze. "I *hoped* it would not…"

They had been walking slowly back and forth, for warmth as much as anything. Now Clara stopped and removed her hand from his arm. "Mr. Weston. Did you really think I was still dangling after Johnathan Mortimer? Did you *really*?"

He tucked his hands under his elbows. "I didn't know."

"Did you not *guess*?"

He looked at her, a smile tugging at his lips. "I don't want to presume. You never told me which way your heart was engaged…"

"Nor did you ask." She waited, raising her brows.

He grinned sheepishly. "Miss Hampton, are you still enamored of that surly, childish scoundrel who's not worthy of holding your shoe?"

She laughed. "I am not, sir. And you're to blame for that."

"I?" He reared back and clapped one bare hand to his chest. Where were his gloves? "How?"

She gave a little shrug, trying not too shiver. It was *cold* out here, but she didn't want to go inside just yet. "By being very good-natured about my brothers and sister teasing you. Mr. Mortimer never would have been so kind to them."

"So you like me because I was kind to your family?"

Clara blushed at his incredulous question. "It helped! But… no. I like you for other reasons, too."

He began to grin. "Do go on."

"You've been rather charming and amusing." She flipped one hand. "Wells is a small town, you know, society is limited."

"So I'm charming compared to the men of Wells?"

"Decidedly."

"That is something," he mused. "Go on."

"Well," she replied, giving him an arch glance. "Handsome, too, now that I think about it."

"Please keep thinking about that," he told her, and she laughed again.

"The answer is that I have not been waiting for Mr. Mortimer for some weeks now," she said. "I cannot tell whether it is good news or bad news that he's run off with some woman from Bath—I suppose it will entertain the matrons of Wells for some time, though. And if the woman from Bath is a scandalous person, Lady Mortimer may not show her face for months, and Sir Eliot's pride will likely be somewhat chastened. But if Mr. Mortimer truly cares for her, and she for him, I suppose it is a good thing, in the end." She wiggled one hand as if weighing the options. "All in all, I think a marriage is better than *bad* news."

Mr. Weston put back his head and laughed. "Thank God!"

Clara smiled. "Have I put your fears to rest?"

"My fears, yes." Still grinning broadly, he put out his hand again. "My hopes, on the other hand, are greatly revived."

"Mr. Weston," she said in mock disappointment, "I begin

to question your intelligence, if your hopes were in such uncertainty." She put her hand in his.

He glanced up at the sky, so dazzling blue he squinted against it. "I was beginning to question my own sanity. But here I am, on Christmas, and I've no gift for you."

"Well," she said after the deliberation of a heartbeat, "you could give me a kiss."

Still squinting at the sky, he smiled. "Miss Hampton. I would like to give you a kiss every morning for the rest of my life."

"That's impertinent," she said.

He glanced at her, his smile fading in surprise.

"You'd have to marry me to do that," she added. "I shan't go around kissing men who are not my husband every morning for the rest of my life. That would be disgraceful."

"No," he said, staring at her. "Would—would you marry me?"

Clara raised her brows. "Just like that?"

"No, no, of course not." He smoothed one hand down his front and cleared his throat. "Miss Hampton, it is my heartfelt desire to call upon you with the most honorable intentions, in the hopes that you might look favorably upon my request, soon to be tendered, for your hand in marriage."

Clara laughed. "Much too pompous! No, you'll have to come in now and have breakfast with my family, and tell my parents your expectations and all that."

"Right now?"

"Yes," she said at his startled expression. "Frightened off already?"

He relaxed and laughed. "Never. And then?"

"Then…. We shall see, hmm?" She smiled brightly at him even as she clutched her shawl tightly, half from cold and half from nerves. What had come over her, to talk to a gentleman this way? She'd all but told him to propose to her.

"Yes, we shall," he murmured, a slow smile spreading over his face again. "But that kiss…"

"Yes," she said breathlessly. "Please."

With a quick glance at the windows behind her, he grabbed her hand and pulled her with him to the shelter of the yew tree beside the house. "Clara," he whispered, his hands on her face.

"Thomas," she said softly. "May I call you that?"

His smile deepened. "Please do," he murmured, and then he kissed her.

Every morning.

For the rest of their lives.

# WHAT HAPPENED NEXT?

Clara and Thomas Weston go on to have three children: James, Abigail, and Penelope. Their stories are part of my Scandals series and can be read in:

It Takes a Scandal (Abigail)
Love in the Time of Scandal (Penelope)
Six Degrees of Scandal (James)

# ...AND TO ALL, A GOOD READ!

If you enjoyed this story, please consider leaving a review online to help other readers. Thank you!

If you would like to get exclusive previews, contests, and my very latest news, join my VIP Readers list at www. CarolineLinden.com. New members also get a free short story as a welcome gift.

# ALSO BY CAROLINE LINDEN

## DESPERATELY SEEKING DUKE

About a Rogue

## THE WAGERS OF SIN

My Once and Future Duke

An Earl Like You

When the Marquess was Mine

## SCANDALS

Love and Other Scandals

It Takes a Scandal

All's Fair in Love and Scandal

Love in the Time of Scandal

A Study in Scandal

Six Degrees of Scandal

The Secret of My Seduction

## THE TRUTH ABOUT THE DUKE

I Love the Earl

One Night in London

Blame It on Bath

The Way to a Duke's Heart

## REECE TRILOGY

What a Gentleman Wants

What a Rogue Desires

A Rake's Guide to Seduction

What a Woman Needs

## NOVELLAS AND COLLECTIONS

*When I Met My Duchess* in At the Duke's Wedding

*Map of a Lady's Heart* in At the Christmas Wedding

*A Fashionable Affair* in Dressed to Kiss

*Will You Be My Wi-Fi?* in At the Billionaire's Wedding

Scandalous Liaisons (boxed set of four novellas)

## SHORT STORIES

A Kiss for Christmas

Like None Other

Written in My Heart

# ABOUT THE AUTHOR

Caroline Linden was born a reader, not a writer. She earned a math degree from Harvard University and wrote computer software before turning to writing fiction. Since then the Boston Red Sox have won the World Series four times, which is not related but still worth mentioning. Her books have been translated into seventeen languages, and have won the NEC Reader's Choice Award, the Daphne du Maurier Award, and RWA's RITA Award.

Visit www.CarolineLinden.com to join her newsletter, and get an exclusive free story just for members.

Made in the USA
Coppell, TX
11 January 2020